GALLAGHER
NOVEL

PULSE
OF MY
HEART

JP O'DONNELL

Outskirts Press, Inc.
http://www.outskirtspress.com

Paperback ISBN: 978-1-9772-0177-5
Hardback ISBN: 978-1-9772-0475-2

Cover Photo © 2018 www.gettyimages.com. Back cover image by AMBI Films , Bent (2018). All rights reserved - used with permission.

Outskirts Press and the "OP" logo are trademarks belonging to Outskirts Press, Inc.

PRINTED IN THE UNITED STATES OF AMERICA

To

Alessandra Eden

Shira Noelani

and

Hasana Rain

Our beautiful granddaughters

Prologue

It happened so fast.

Don Kraemer was jogging along the dirt path of the Wabash Heritage Trail that led through the woods on a four-mile trek to an old, iron-truss bridge that crossed the Wabash River. The trail was empty today; no other joggers or walkers in sight. But that's how he liked it.

Solitude.

No distractions.

A quiet escape.

A chance to be alone and try to resolve the issues that had come up during the previous week.

Issues. There were always issues.

Could he afford to expand his landscaping business by adding another truck? What about a private school for Hayley? God knows, it would help her to overcome her shyness.

"Selective mutism" the doctor called it.

But $15,000 a year for nursery school and tutors? Where will the money come from?

He continued running and thinking, but no solutions came to mind.

Then, a rustling noise from the bushes along the trail startled him.

He stopped and turned toward the sound. The rustling became a loud, angry growl.

Don twisted to his left and instinctively raised his right arm to defend his face.

Too late—the bushes exploded with a roar, and a white pit bull leaped toward him. Its mouth was open and foaming, and vicious teeth were directed at Don's neck.

The dog's front paws felt like clubs as they pounded his body and knocked him off balance and down to the ground. Don's left hip slammed onto a rock on the side of the dirt path.

Pain shot through his leg.

He rolled onto his back.

He flailed his arms, trying to fight off this beast that thrashed and growled while attacking him. Don felt a searing pain as the dog's teeth fastened on his arm like a vise.

The dog persisted with its mauling attack like an out-of-control motor—scratching, biting, and slobbering its spittle all over Don's face and neck. Stunned and overmatched, Don made a futile effort to resist the powerful animal. He tried to scream for help, but his fall had taken his breath away. The only sound he could muster was a faint grunt.

All of his strength and energy concentrated on nothing else but survival. He squeezed his eyes shut to avoid having them scratched out, but then he was forced to fight back blindly—he knew he was helpless. He began to slip into a state of shock.

My God! I'm going to die here!

"Caesar—Stop!" a man's voice boomed from behind the trail, followed by the sound of rapidly approaching footsteps.

"No!—Stop!—No!" the man screamed as he grabbed the dog's collar and pulled the thrashing animal away from Don's chest. He struggled to restrain the dog from attacking again. The dog twisted and turned wildly and reared up on its hind legs in an attempt to break loose and make another charge at its prey.

Don's heart, which had seemed to stop beating when the dog first appeared, now pounded uncontrollably. Dazed, he crawled up on all fours, fought to regain his breath, and then rose to his feet, thankful to still be alive but overwhelmed by anger at the dog's owner.

How could someone let an animal like this get off its leash? he thought.

Beads of sweat gathered on his forehead; blood trickled down from the dozens of scratches on his neck and face. He glanced at his forearm where fresh puncture wounds were already discolored to dark purple and surrounded by long, linear scratches, which provided clear evidence of the dog's ferocious attack and sharp teeth.

"Your dog—your dog almost killed me!" Don shouted.

His voice quivered, and he gasped for breath.

"Sorry, man. He break off his leash. I chase after him as fas' as I can," the man said with a Latino accent.

He almost lost his breath himself as he fought to gain control of the dog. He was short in stature but displayed considerable strength as both of his hands tightly gripped the dog's collar. He flexed his knees, dug his heels into the ground, and leaned back, restraining the wild creature whose front legs flailed about in a useless attempt to gain traction and attack again.

The man repeatedly slapped the back of the dog's head and screamed, "No, Caesar—No!"

The blows to his head got the pit bull's attention, and with a piercing yelp, he finally became submissive. The man reached into his pocket and pulled out a braided nylon leash. He attached the leash to the dog's collar and secured it to the trunk of a small maple tree.

"Stay!—Stay!" he repeated loudly as he pointed at the pit bull with his right hand and stared directly into its face.

The dog panted heavily and was still excited but sat down and dutifully obeyed its master.

The man turned his attention back to Don and walked closer.

"I'm so sorry, man. You okay?"

Then, tilting his head to look at the right side of Don's face, he curled his lower lip, shrugged his shoulders, and added, "Look like you just got a few scratches here. You be okay."

"What about this bite on my arm?" asked Don, displaying the purple puncture marks on his right arm.

"No—no worry, sir. My dog not sick. I take him to vet all the time. He have all his shots. No problem for you. Your arm will be better in no time."

A wide, gap-toothed smile flashed across his round face in an attempt to reassure his battered accuser.

Don wasn't buying his glib attitude.

"Not so fast. This fuckin' dog is dangerous. What if a woman or some little kid was running along here? He would have killed them! I'm reporting this to the police."

"Easy, man—easy," the man said, raising his hands in front of his chest in a conciliatory manner and glancing back to make sure that the pit bull remained tethered.

"If you tell the police, they put my dog to sleep. This not his fault."

Then, pointing to his chest, he added, "My fault he get off his leash. He a good dog. Don't punish him for my mistake."

He undid a thick, gold necklace from around his neck and offered it to Don. "Here, man. You take this for your trouble. It worth more than one thousand dollar. You don't report my dog. You keep the necklace. I make sure he don't bother nobody ever again."

The man raised his eyebrows and nodded toward Don, begging him to accept the offer.

"I don't want your fuckin' necklace. I just want your name and the name of your veterinarian so I can make sure this beast has had his shots."

Don looked down at his arms and torn shirt, still trying to determine the extent of his wounds.

The man shook his head, sighed, and retreated. Realizing the futility of his offer, he slipped the necklace into his pocket. He looked away for an instant as if contemplating his next peace offering.

"Okay, man. You have some paper? I give you my name and

the number."

Having somewhat regained his composure but still highly agitated, Don snarled, "I don't usually carry paper and a pen when I'm out jogging. Give me the information and I'll put it into my cell phone."

He reached into his pants pocket.

Empty.

He had left his cell phone on the front seat of his car.

"Shit!" he muttered to himself and looked up to the sky and chastised himself for this dumb mistake that could prove costly.

The man recognized Don's dilemma immediately and pulled out his own cell phone.

"No problem, man. We call your phone and I leave my name and vet's number in your message box. Okay?"

He held the phone out toward Don and smiled.

Don grabbed the cell phone and punched in his number. Don slapped the phone back into the hand of the short-statured man who continued smiling gratuitously. This guy's "suck-up" approach only increased Don's irritation.

The little man looked toward Don who seemed preoccupied with the wounds on his right arm that he studied intently. The little man then turned away, slyly punched a few number keys on his phone, looked down at the ground, and tucked his chin into his chest as he spoke into the phone.

"My name is Diego Rivera. 450 Mosely Road, West Lafayette. My dog's vet is River Valley Animal Hospital. (682) 555-1020," he said as if reading a script.

Then he flipped the phone closed and shoved it back into

his front pants pocket.

"You call later," he said. "I very sorry my dog hurt you, but you see, everythin' be okay. If you see doctor, I pay your bill. Just let me know—okay?"

Now quite animated in his actions, he took several steps backward while he was talking. Then he turned to his dog, untied the leash from the tree, and hurriedly made his way through the bushes and down a slight incline. The pit bull ran ahead of him, practically pulling the leash out of his hand.

Don watched them scamper down the hill toward a beat-up, dark-blue pickup truck—a Toyota Tacoma—parked in a clearing that opened to a dirt road leading back to State Road 42.

Now in a near sprint, Diego reached the waiting Tacoma truck and opened the rear passenger door. The driver, wearing a red baseball cap, leaned out the window and glanced back at Don. The pit bull jumped in. Diego closed the rear door and quickly got into the front passenger seat. The man in the driver's seat stared back at Don with a menacing look while the driver side window slowly closed.

The driver turned toward Diego and spoke in an angry tone. "I'm gonna kill that fuckin' dog! The last thing we need is a set of eyes watching us!"

"He never did anything like this before. Maybe he's sick? I'll have the vet check him out. Don't worry ... that Gringo won't be a problem."

The driver ignored his plea. "I'm tellin' you ... that fuckin' dog is a problem. I'm gonna kill the sonovabitch,"

Diego suddenly lunged toward the driver, holding a six-inch knife to his throat. Taken by surprise, the driver leaned back against the side window and lifted his head upward in a desperate attempt to avoid the sharp blade.

His eyes widened in fear.

He tried to speak but couldn't get any words out as the blade slightly pierced the skin below his chin, drawing blood in the process.

Diego spoke to him with a venomous whisper, "You lay a hand on my dog and I'll slit your fuckin' throat."

The driver struggled to lift his head higher, as his neck strained to escape the piercing blade and a state of panic set in.

Then with a wild-eyed menacing look, Diego pushed in closer, within an inch of the driver's face.

"Or maybe I cut off your balls and feed them to my dog," he said.

Diego then relaxed his grip on the driver's shoulder and slowly withdrew the knife. Then he placed it into a scabbard on the right side of his belt.

The driver quickly ran his left hand under his chin, saw the blood and wiped it on his pants while staring straight ahead. He settled back behind the steering wheel without saying a word.

Unaware of the scene that had just unfolded inside the truck, Don continued to peer down at the clearing and saw a second vehicle driving away, having reached the junction with the main road. As this car made a left turn, Don squinted to be sure he wasn't mistaken. The car was black and had dark tinted windows. The side mirrors and the base of the rear windshield had emergency lights. A radio antenna extended up from the trunk.

It was an unmarked police car.

Within seconds, the Tacoma truck had also sped away.

Don surveyed the scene, still shocked and confused by the experience. He leaned down and brushed the dust and debris off his running shorts and legs. The pain in his hip made him wince. The scratches on his face stung from the sweat and dirt that had seeped into the crevices of the broken skin. His right arm throbbed at the site of the puncture wound.

As he limped along toward the beginning of the trail, he wondered, *What the hell was going on here?*

Chapter 1

Emptiness.

Daniel Cormac Gallagher, Jr. could find no other word to describe his feelings. It had been eight months since Kate left him, on the heels of yet another attempt on his life—an attempt that had, once again, drawn her into his dangerous world as a Boston private eye.

Kathryn Daisy McSurdy—her Irish-green name resonated in his mind.

Her image was fixed and untarnished.

Simply stated—a knockout.

But there was so much more to Kate than just good looks. She had an inner strength—a redoubtable toughness—that surfaced whenever she faced a crisis. Most of the time she managed to keep it out of the view of her friends and family, but Gallagher could always sense its presence.

He knew he could count on her always—in so many ways.

Yet, she managed to blend the toughness with genuine sensitivity and compassion. She could watch a report about a drunken driver who had caused a fatal accident, and while sympathizing with the victims, she could find a place in her heart for the family of the driver. Did he have a mother, a brother, or a sister who loved him? Someone who had always believed in him? Someone who had tried to make a difference but hadn't been able to reach him?

These were among Kate's warmest inner qualities that far surpassed those of her exquisite exterior.

But he had let her get away.

How did it happen?

Day after day, he asked himself the same question.

It wasn't his fault entirely, but he had to shoulder most of the blame. After all, his choice of dangerous assignments—the ones he could never seem to resist—had made her an innocent victim of ruthless criminals who were determined to attain their objectives no matter who got in their way.

Kate's life had been threatened on two occasions, and she had been present at the scene of three deaths, all by gunshot wounds. During her time with Gallagher, she had endured a home invasion in which a man had held a gun to her head while waiting to assassinate Gallagher. Thanks to her quick thinking—again, the redoubtable toughness—and Gallagher's considerable skill with a gun, they had survived.

He had promised to pursue a safer line of work.

Within a year they had married, and their life together had been filled with happiness and bright horizons. She had begged him to move on—to give up his career as a private investigator.

Despite the promise, he couldn't do it.

Or, maybe "wouldn't" was the operative word.

Gallagher took on another case—"Just one more," as he had

described it—but it was a decision that had proven to be a near fatal mistake. He had investigated a car-bombing incident and the disappearance of a mysterious woman. It had seemed like a simple assignment, but, before he knew it, he had become embroiled in solving a complex, treasonous plot to sell secret code-breaking formulas to North Korea. As he got closer to the truth, he had become a target of those who wanted to silence him.

At the same time, the Las Vegas mob had plans to dispose of him. They were eager to settle an old score and prevent him from revealing the truth about a bribery case involving a United States congressman. Two men had been dispatched by a Vegas underworld boss to kill Gallagher. Once again, he had survived, but only after Kate had fired three shots into the back of a hit man—the man who was about to end Gallagher's life.

It had all been too much for her.

She was scarred by the incidents with guns and feared that her relationship with Gallagher would either place her in danger again or, at the very least, make her a widow. Kate had had enough.

She was the one who had to move on.

Their divorce had been quick, but amicable. Gallagher continued to respect her wishes for privacy and had not seen or spoken to her in more than six months.

Now, at age forty-seven, he faced the challenge of picking up the pieces of his screwed-up life. On the scoreboard of marriages, Gallagher had become a two-time loser. Only this time his recovery seemed full of doubt.

Moving on?

How was it possible when most of your waking thoughts turned to the once-in-a-lifetime woman who you had let get away?

He had heard all the stories about "starting over." It was supposed to be so much easier for men: just go to a few bars—or sign up for a dating service—and pick up the chicks.

Not interested.

Instead he found himself drinking too much coffee.

And, yes—way too much Scotch. You know things are tough when you drink alone.

It was not so easy after all. Most nights he was plain miserable and hardly slept. He couldn't stop recalling how Kate had held his hand across a table or the passion of her kisses.

He had become convinced that women get over a break-up much easier.

For men, it's like slow death.

———◦((◦))◦———

Sitting in his Commercial Street office, Gallagher shuffled through the papers on his desk trying to get his mind off Kate and back to the business of being a private investigator. He reviewed a stack of medical insurance bills filed by a guy who claimed to be disabled, but the insurance company that hired Gallagher suspected a phony claim. Gallagher's job was to follow this guy to determine if his disability was valid.

These insurance fraud cases were lucrative for Gallagher,

but he hated them nonetheless. At times, he felt like he was wrecking too many lives—snooping around on behalf of some billion-dollar company and digging up dirt on some little guy.

He much preferred cases like the one involving Camara Watkins, a sixteen-year-old girl who had run away with her "bad-ass" boyfriend. The girl's parents wanted to keep the story away from the police and the newspapers, so they hired Gallagher—well known by lawyers in Boston for his ability to find runaways and bring them home safely.

Luckily, he had received a good lead. Camara's aunt, who lived next door to Camara's family, had discovered that one of her credit cards was missing, and she phoned Diane Beane, Gallagher's secretary, who then obtained a printout of the credit card statement. Diane circled the recent transactions, all of which had taken place in New Haven, Connecticut, and the printout was in Gallagher's pocket as he drove from Boston to New Haven. He intended to stake out a Starbucks Coffee Shop where the stolen card had been used several times.

For a man with a genuine addiction to coffee, the hours of waiting had hardly strained his patience. But the real bonus occurred when Gallagher spotted the girl and persuaded her to come home to her family. These cases provided the emotional reward he valued; insurance fraud cases paid the rent.

Gallagher studied the list of insurance claims, all the while rolling a coin—a 1937 Irish half-crown—across the fingers of his right hand. The coin had been a gift from his grandfather. He often used it to practice the coin-rolling and sleight-of-hand skills that he had learned when he studied magic as a teenager. On occasion, Gallagher's adeptness in sleight-of-hand, as well as another favorite—lock-picking—proved invaluable in securing a clue or a piece of evidence for cases he investigated.

Gallagher leaned back and placed his feet up on the dark mahogany desk. He stretched out his trim six-foot frame and flexed his back and stomach muscles—part of his daily routine to strengthen his core.

Just after one-thirty, the phone rang. Diane's voice came over the intercom. "Dan, do you have a minute to speak to Bob McSurdy?"

Bob McSurdy?

Kate's father?

Why would he be calling me?

Gallagher picked up the phone. "Bob? How are you?"

"I'm alright, I guess. But I'm worried about something…I'd like to talk to you. Can we get together sometime?"

"Sure. Anytime. What's wrong?"

"It's about Kate…"

A long pause.

Gallagher didn't like the direction this conversation had suddenly taken. Then, his heart dropped when Bob finished his sentence.

"I'm afraid something's happened to her. She's missing."

Chapter 2

Bob McSurdy's phone call had sent Gallagher's head into a tailspin. He had asked Bob for more specifics, but Bob had begged off, preferring to speak to Gallagher in person.

Within an hour, Bob arrived at Gallagher's office. He exchanged several uneasy pleasantries with Diane, then walked in and sat down across from Gallagher's desk. Gallagher immediately noticed the puffiness beneath Bob's sagging eyes. His thinning gray hair, usually combed meticulously in place, was parted unevenly, and a few long strands haphazardly drooped over his right ear.

The poor guy looked like he needed a good night's sleep.

"Can I get something for you, Bob? Coffee or a cold drink?" asked Gallagher, whose five-second assessment told him that Bob was indeed under a considerable amount of stress.

"No—nothing. I've already had lunch. I'm all set," said Bob.

He shifted his shoulders and fidgeted with his fingers on the arms of the chair.

Gallagher leaned forward, placed his hands together, and his elbows on the desk. "Okay, then—let's not waste any time. What's happened to Kate? What makes you think she's missing?"

"Well, it's sort of complicated. I know you two are divorced, but I also know you still care about each other. I wish things were different—that you were still together— but—"His voice trailed off as he searched for the words.

"Thanks Bob. I wish they could be different myself."

Bob gathered himself and spoke with a newfound authority.

"I'm here because I don't have anyone else to turn to. The police won't listen."

Gallagher held his hand out as if making a stop signal and flashed a quick smile. "Hold on, Bob, please. Let's start from the very beginning."

Bob inhaled deeply and shook his head.

"Sorry. I'm all worked up. Barbara's beside herself with worry. She couldn't bring herself to come down here today."

"Okay, you're here now. Try to relax and give me the details."

"Two weeks ago, Kate called us and said she had to make a trip out to Indiana. My niece, Cindy, had lost her husband unexpectedly. Young man—terrible thing. Died from some acute infection that overtook his body."

"That's awful. What happened?"

"I don't know the particulars. We wanted to go with her, but Barbara's been under the weather and couldn't make the trip."

"What's wrong with Barbara?"

"She had a bad bout with the flu; then came down with pneumonia."

"I'm sorry to hear that."

"Yes, thanks. She almost ended up in the hospital. But the antibiotics finally kicked in, and she's been getting better. Until this."

Gallagher shifted topics from his former mother-in-law's medical status, trying to get back to the main story.

"I never heard Kate mention Cindy. How is she related?" he asked.

"She's the daughter of Barbara's oldest brother. He passed away about ten years ago. His wife, Gilda, remarried and moved to Florida, so we don't see her very often. We kind of lost contact with Cindy after she moved to Indiana and got married. She's a few years younger than Kate. I'm surprised you haven't heard her name from Kate. After all—"

Bob paused, seemingly at a loss for words again. He put his head down for a few seconds, trying to gather himself again to continue speaking. Gallagher noticed a tremor in his hands.

Is this something new? The guy is falling apart. Could it all be from stress?

Gallagher ignored Bob's last comment regarding Kate's cousin and tried to keep pushing for the specifics.

"So, Kate went out to Indiana for the funeral?"

"Actually, she went out a few days after the funeral. You know, her agreement with Cindy all along had been to limit the contact with her. They agreed that it would be best for all concerned."

Gallagher's frustration with this conversation had reached the point of exasperation.

"Bob, you're losing me here. What agreement are you talking about?"

"You mean, Kate never told you?"

"Told me about what?"

"The baby—Kate's baby. Cindy and her husband, Don, adopted Kate's baby."

Chapter 3

In Gallagher's career as a private investigator, he had encountered many shocking revelations—confessions, clues, uncovered pieces of evidence or, at times, a twist in a case that had taken him by surprise. But the news that Kate had a baby left him wounded and practically speechless.

How is this possible? I thought I knew everything about her.

Gallagher slipped back in his chair and shook his head. He looked directly at Bob, whose own perplexed look added to the increasingly uncomfortable feeling that pervaded the office.

Had someone sucked the air out of the room?

"No, Bob. I know nothing about a baby. Kate never shared that information with me."

"I'm sorry. I thought for sure you knew," Bob said, as he looked away for a few seconds, diverting his eyes from Gallagher's unwavering stare.

"That doesn't matter now. Just tell me how all of this fits into Kate's disappearance," said Gallagher.

"Before Kate met you she was involved with a Patriots' football player, Matt Winston. They were together for almost four years."

"Winston? Don't remember him."

"Part-time linebacker—special teams guy." Bob shook his head. "Not one of their big stars."

"Okay."

"Well, things were fine while he was still playing, but after he retired, his mean streak seemed to come out. Sometimes I think it was the steroids. Who knows? A lot of those guys took them."

Bob heaved a big sigh and swallowed hard. The pain of re-living this sorry episode in his daughter's life was obvious.

"His temper tantrums kept getting worse. I think Kate was ready to break things off with him. One night, when she came home from her office, he was in a foul mood. I think he be-gan to sense that she wanted out of the relationship. He forced himself on her. She told us she tried to resist him, but then gave in to avoid getting hurt."

"You mean he raped her?"

"Yes," said Bob angrily. "I swear—when she told me, I want-ed to kill the sonovabitch."

Bob's right hand clenched into a tight fist. He pursed his lips together and lowered his head.

"I just …" he started and then stopped, unable to finish his thought. His eyes welled up. His long-suppressed anger had worked its way to the surface.

Gallagher tried to keep his own anger under control and offered some words of support.

"I know just how you feel, Bob. I would have wanted to kill him myself."

Bob looked up with steely resolve.

"You know—so many things came out about this guy after his football career was over. I only wish we had known sooner. He started out as such a nice guy but then seemed to turn into a dangerous bully. He got into a few fights with teammates—punched out the trainer one time. Real anger management issues. No wonder the team got rid of him. But all of it was hushed up. Near the end, Kate began to see the changes, but by the time she decided to get out of the relationship, it was too late."

Gallagher looked away for a few seconds and tried to sort out his own feelings of shock and anger.

"Kate never told me about the abuse. I wish I had known."

Then, he looked back to Bob and tried to push him for the rest of the story.

"What happened after he assaulted Kate?" he asked.

"Kate knew I was hot—ready to go after him. But she insisted that I stay out of it. She got a restraining order against him and moved out. But even with the restraining order I still worry about that guy. He can be dangerous."

Gallagher nodded his head and raised his eyebrows.

"I think I know what's coming next."

"Yes," said Bob. "Two months later Kate found out she was pregnant."

"Did she tell Matt?"

"No, she wanted him completely out of her life. If he had known about the baby, he could have filed for joint custody. She would have never been able to get rid of him."

"Knowing Kate, an abortion was out of the question," said Gallagher.

"That's right. An abortion just went totally against her grain. She wanted to have the baby but give it up for adoption to a good family."

"So that's where Cindy came in?"

"Yes. Kate heard Barbara mention that Cindy and Don had been married for a while and were unable to have their own children. Kate really hadn't had much contact with Cindy over the years. Cindy's a few years younger than Kate, but they always got along well when they were growing up as cousins. So, she contacted Cindy and flew out to Indiana to meet with her and Don."

This tedious rehashing of the story was making Gallagher impatient. He needed to know how Kate had suddenly gone missing.

He sat up and encouraged Bob to speed things up, "All right, so Kate had the baby and gave it to them—"

"It wasn't so simple," Bob said. "Kate had a business to take care of. Her partner, Ellie, knew about the recent break-up with Matt and accepted the fact that Kate needed to get away from him for a while. Ellie agreed to cover the business for six months. Kate also wanted to make sure that no one knew she was pregnant for fear that the news would get back to Matt. So she moved out to Indiana during her third month and stayed there until the baby was delivered. They worked everything out with the social services agency so that the adoption became legal in Indiana.

"The baby's name is Hayley. She's three years old now. Everything was fine until two weeks ago, when we got the call about Don's death. Kate spoke to Cindy for a long while. She said Cindy was under enormous stress and confused about a lot of things surrounding Don's death. So Kate flew out there to give her some support. This was going to be the first time Kate would see Hayley since the day she was born."

"Then what happened?" asked Gallagher.

"Kate called us every day for the first week, but then the calls stopped. We've tried calling her cell phone, but it never answers. We figured she was having a problem with her phone and tried calling Cindy's house. But we get nothing but the answering machine. We haven't heard anything from anyone for five days."

"Did you try calling the local police in Indiana?"

"They live in a small town called Townsend. It's near Lafayette. I called the Townsend police and asked them to check the house. They called back and said no one was home but everything was in order. They thought maybe Cindy and Kate had taken Hayley away for a few days."

"I doubt that," said Gallagher. "Not without notifying you."

"I agree. I tried telling the police the same thing and asked if I could file a missing-persons report. But they said people have the right to go off by themselves. There must be a reason to suspect that they are in danger, otherwise the police don't get involved. I can't imagine what could have happened to them. But I'm worried sick about it."

Gallagher seized upon one of Bob's earlier comments.

"You said Cindy was confused about some of the things surrounding Don's death. Did Kate give you any specifics about that?"

"No, she just said a lot of things didn't add up and that Cindy was still trying to get some answers. She did say that Cindy had a few discussions with the police, but they weren't very helpful."

Shaking his head, he said, "I can see why it was so hard for her to accept his death. Such a young man. Ran a landscaping business. He was only about forty-five."

Gallagher's voice perked up, "Cindy talked with the police? I thought you said Don died from some kind of infection. Why would she be talking to the police instead of his doctors?"

"I don't know. I wondered the same, but Kate never elaborated very much. I think she didn't want us to worry about what was going on out there. In the end, though, all Barbara and I have done is worry. There's something not right about this whole thing."

Gallagher sat motionless, trying to consider all of the facts he'd just heard, while his mind simultaneously churned about what he should do.

Bob looked across the desk and interrupted Gallagher's thoughts.

Bob's eyes were moist, and his voice cracked with emotion as he spoke, "Like I said—I had to call you. I didn't know where else to turn. You find a lot of missing people in your line of work, don't you? What can you do to find Kate?"

Gallagher didn't answer.

But there was something he did know for sure—he was on his way to Indiana.

Chapter 4

Five nights earlier.

State Trooper Mike DelPeschio slowed down, put on his cruiser's flashing lights, and pulled into the breakdown lane on State Road 5 near Lafayette, Indiana. He noted the time—2:23 am.

He had drawn the late shift this week, 11:00 pm to 7:00 am. At these late hours, he never knew what he would encounter on a given night—DUIs, head-on collisions, abandoned cars that had run out of gas.

It was an endless list of possibilities.

But in the distance off to his right, as he passed the intersection with Willard Road, he had just seen black smoke and a flash of fire.

He knew this could be serious.

He made a quick "U" turn as he spoke into the hand-held microphone of his police car radio, "Unit Number Nine responding to an apparent fire in the brush on Willard Road off State Road 5. Notify the fire department."

The brief sound of static was followed by the voice of a

female dispatcher, "10-4, Unit Nine. Fire department notified and responding."

DelPeschio turned up Willard Road and stepped on the accelerator. About a half-mile ahead he could see billows of smoke and the flicker of flames. As he drew closer, he saw a smoldering car that had rolled off the road and down a short embankment into a cluster of trees. The car was lying on the driver side with the wheels of the passenger side completely off the ground. The passenger cabin appeared crushed by the roof of the car.

"Unit Number Nine on scene," DelPeschio called into his mobile shoulder mic as he opened his door. "I have an overturned vehicle on fire. Unknown if the vehicle is occupied. The vehicle is at the bottom of a short embankment off the side of the road. Requesting additional trooper units and an ambulance to respond."

He got out of his cruiser and carefully worked his way down the embankment toward the smoking vehicle.

"Anyone in there?" he yelled. "Hello! Hello! Can anyone hear me? Help is on the way," he called out again.

No answer.

He crawled up a small incline so he could shine his flashlight into the passenger cabin through the shattered windshield. He could see the outline of a person slumped in the driver's seat, being held there by the vehicle's safety harness. There was no movement. He could see the distorted remnants of a child's car seat in the back.

It was empty.

There was no way for DelPeschio to enter the smoking wreckage to determine if there were any survivors or if the person in the driver's seat was dead or alive.

DelPeschio radioed to Dispatch, "There is only one occupant visible in the vehicle. The occupant is motionless and unresponsive. Obvious burn wounds. Possible fatality. An extrication team will be required to enter the vehicle and access the victim."

The sound of sirens grew louder. Two fire trucks, an ambulance, an extrication team, and a state police car arrived on the scene. The firefighters worked feverishly to extinguish the fire.

DelPeschio and the other state trooper quickly spread out to scour the surrounding area with their flashlights in a search for any additional victims. As seasoned veterans of the State Highway Patrol they knew that accidents of this sort could cause a passenger to be ejected from a vehicle and be found lying on the ground nearby.

Twigs and branches cracked beneath their feet as they trampled through the underbrush.

Finally, the other trooper looked over at DelPeschio.

"Nothing, Mike," he said.

DelPeschio gave him a deadpanned look and a one-word reply.

"Right."

Within a few minutes, the fire was extinguished. With the vehicle still lying on the driver's side, the extrication team went into action. Using wooden chocks and heavy-duty extrication straps, the team worked quickly to secure the vehicle and prevent it from rolling over. As DelPeschio watched the team use the Jaws of Life to enter the passenger cabin, he noticed that the license plate number of the car was still legible.

"On this Willard Road MVA, we've got Indiana plates. Seven, Charlie, Mary, Zebra, Nine, Five. Copy?" he said into his mobile.

"Indiana Seven, Charlie, Mary, Zebra, Nine, Five," replied the dispatcher.

"10-4," said DelPeschio.

As he spoke, DelPeschio could see the paramedics shaking their heads as they checked the victim's lifeless body for a pulse.

"Unit Number Nine. Single occupant. Confirmed fatality. Please notify the medical examiner. Awaiting positive ID," he said into his radio.

DelPeschio walked over toward the smoldering car. He had a pained expression on his face as he looked at the victim.

A few seconds later, the dispatcher's voice responded, "10-4, Unit Number Nine.

"10-4," said DelPeschio.

"10-4. Over."

Chapter 5

As the grapefruit came tumbling down the display case and rolled off the edge, he reached out and snatched it before it landed on the floor.

"Nice save! With reflexes like that, you should still be sacking quarterbacks," a woman's voice called from across the aisle.

Matt Winston looked up in surprise at a smiling woman with a round face and short brown hair. A pair of oversized sunglasses rested on the top of her head. She looked familiar, but Matt had no clue about her name.

"Thanks," he said, almost embarrassed by the attention. "You must be a Pats fan."

"Damn right! Season-ticket holder," she said proudly. "You were always one of my favorites."

"Thanks, again." He extended his hand, "Sorry, you look very familiar, but I don't remember your name."

"Ginny Dutkevich. Nice to see you again, Matt. I used to work for Dr. Garcia-Rogers, Kate's doctor. But now I'm with the Kaufman Management Group. Better hours; better benefits," she said.

She smiled and shrugged her shoulders.

"Oh, yes. Now I remember. Kate mentioned you a few times. Didn't she introduce us at the End Zone lounge after one of the games?"

"Hey, good memory! Glad to see you're back in this area."

"Yes," said Matt, confused by her comment, but letting it slip by.

The conversation was growing uncomfortable, and he sought a way to escape.

"In fact, when Kate requested that her records be transferred to an obstetrician in the Midwest, I figured you had taken a coaching job out there," Ginny continued.

"Midwest?" said Matt.

"Yeah, wasn't it Lafayette, Indiana, or somewhere in that area? I did all the paper work, assembling the lab reports and ultrasound results. I remember thinking at the time that you must have taken a job with the Colts or some college team. Did you guys move out there for a while?" she asked, beginning to be puzzled herself by the blank look on Matt's face.

Matt paused for a few seconds, licked his lower lip, and exhaled deeply. "Actually, Ginny—Kate and I aren't together anymore. It's been awhile."

Realizing her blunder, she gasped and covered her mouth with her right hand.

"Oh, my god! I'm terribly sorry. I just assumed you two had gotten married. Guess I spoke out of turn. You were together for such a long time while you were playing."

Then, she stomped her foot, "Damn! Talk about violating the HIPPA laws and putting your foot in your mouth, Ginny."

Matt's thoughts were racing, but he tried to appear gracious so he could extricate himself from this increasingly awkward chance encounter.

"No problem, Ginny. You had no way of knowing." Then, he flipped the grapefruit into his shopping cart and said, "Look, it was nice seeing you again. I'm meeting up with some friends later, so I've gotta run."

He turned away and hustled the cart out of the produce aisle toward the cash registers in the front of the store. He glanced back toward Ginny. She had turned her attention to the fruit on the display stand and was idly sorting through the apples.

Now consumed with anger, Matt shoved the shopping cart toward a side aisle where it slammed into an end display of canned goods and sending more than a dozen cans to crash loudly to the floor. The sudden noise startled an elderly woman who lurched back from her shopping cart and twisted her ankle in the process. She stumbled, lost her balance, and fell to the floor. Matt ignored the plight of the injured woman and walked away, leaving his groceries inside the cart.

He stormed through the exit of the supermarket, swearing to himself as he approached his car.

Obstetrician? Now I know why I couldn't find her for months. I'll get even with her.

That was my baby! And she took it away so I'd never see it!

Chapter 6

Gallagher wanted to get to Kate's last known location in Indiana as soon as possible. Unfortunately, Bob's visit had come too late in the day. The best that Diane could arrange was a nonstop flight on Delta that landed in Indianapolis at 11:56 am the next morning. He wanted to fly directly to Lafayette, but there was no nonstop service from Boston. Gallagher's present state of mind offered little tolerance for time-wasting layovers.

Within minutes of claiming his single piece of luggage in Indianapolis, he whisked his way through the terminal, grabbed a rental from Budget, and drove off on the sixty-mile trip to Townsend, a town northwest of Lafayette. A little over an hour later, he parked in front of a ranch style home at 1301 Bates Avenue, on the corner of Atwood Street in Townsend. The address had been given to him by Bob McSurdy. It was the home of Don and Cindy Kraemer—the last place where Kate was known to have been.

Gallagher made a quick survey of the area.

A quiet residential neighborhood with modest-sized homes.

Bates Avenue had more traffic than Atwood since it connected to Main Street, which had an on/off connection to the

Interstate about a mile and a half away. He noticed a police cruiser parked on Atwood about one hundred feet away from the Kraemer home.

Gallagher walked up the driveway and then up two short steps to an alcove in front of the main entrance. He noticed a wheelchair ramp that gradually led from the driveway with a slight incline all the way to the front door.

Does a disabled person live in this house? he wondered.

He also noticed that the mailbox was jammed so full that the lid barely managed to close. He counted six newspapers lying on the stoop. Bob McSurdy's timetable appeared to be accurate—no one had been home for the past six days. Gallagher didn't expect an answer, but he rang the doorbell nevertheless. The house remained quiet; no one answered. He turned away from the front door, and slipped between two azalea bushes to peer into one of the two dining-room windows, hoping to see something that might provide a clue about the inhabitants. He lifted up on his toes, and put his hands over his eyes to block the glare from the window glass.

A booming voice from behind startled him, "Stop right there! Keep your hands above your head and turn around slowly."

Gallagher froze.

Then he made a careful pivot, turning slowly and catching a view of a young police officer standing on the lawn with his gun drawn, pointing it directly at Gallagher's chest.

"Who are you? What business do you have at this house?" shouted the officer.

Now facing him directly, Gallagher replied calmly, "Easy does it, Officer. The name's Gallagher; I'm a private investigator from Boston. I've been sent here by relatives of the owners to find out why they haven't responded to any of their calls."

"Just keep your hands up," said the officer. "Now turn around again and face the house."

Gallagher dutifully obeyed, thinking to himself, *I hope this kid isn't trigger happy.*

"All right, now put your hands down and place them behind your back"

"I can show you my ID, Officer, if it will help to verify my story," he said, trying to defuse the situation.

But there was no response—just the clicking sounds from a pair of handcuffs that were secured around his wrists.

Then the officer began a monotoned recitation of a phrase all too familiar to Gallagher. "You have the right to remain silent. Anything you say or do can and will be held against you in a court of law. You have the right to speak to an attorney. If you cannot afford an attorney, one will be appointed for you. Do you understand these rights as they have been read to you?"

Gallagher had been in Indiana for less than two hours, and he was already under arrest.

Chapter 7

The ride in the back of the police cruiser was not exactly a pleasant sightseeing tour of the Indiana town. Without speaking a word to his captive, the young officer had thrown Gallagher's suitcase into the front seat and then radioed to the main station that he had taken a prowler at the Kraemer residence into custody.

"You have a nice way of greeting folks from out of town. Is this what the Chamber of Commerce recommends to make us feel welcome around here?" asked Gallagher, trying to get a smile out of this stiff.

The deadpanned officer continued driving and stared at the road ahead.

"Save it for the Captain," he said. "You'll have plenty of time to give your story to him."

After a fifteen-minute ride with no further conversation, the police cruiser pulled up to a red-brick building with a precast-stone front bearing a sign, "Townsend Police Station." The officer, holding Gallagher's suitcase in one hand, opened the rear door and motioned to Gallagher to get out.

Gallagher reached up, handed the handcuffs to the officer,

and said, "Here you go. You might need these for the next guy you take into custody."

Dumbfounded, the officer studied the handcuffs as Gallagher swung his legs out to the ground and lifted himself out of the car. Still perplexed by Gallagher's escape, the officer grabbed Gallagher by the arm and pulled him toward the entrance.

"Come with me, wise guy," he said.

Gallagher merely smiled and offered no resistance.

Inside the police station, the officer bypassed the booking area and escorted Gallagher directly to an office located at the end of a short hallway. As they entered the office, a uniformed man with a neatly-trimmed mustache straightened up in his chair behind a desk that bore a sign "Captain James Hartman." His short-cropped hair had sprinkles of gray—an indication that he had experience as well as rank. His piercing eyes met Gallagher's in an instant.

He stood up quickly, put his hands on his hips like a Marine drill sergeant, and wasted no time getting to the point.

"Just what were you doing at the Kraemer house?" he barked.

"Looking for Cindy Kraemer and my ex-wife, Kate Gall—I mean Kate McSurdy," Gallagher stammered, still getting used to the fact that Kate had gone back to her maiden name after the divorce.

"What was your ex-wife doing here?"

"She's Cindy's cousin from Boston."

"You said ex-wife. Why would you be looking for your ex-wife?"

"She came out to visit Cindy. Her parents haven't heard from her in six days and asked me to find her."

Hartman veered away from his brusque line of questioning, darted a stare at the young officer who was trying to play the good soldier by standing at attention next to Gallagher.

Hartman snapped, "You picked this man up for prowling. Why isn't he cuffed?"

"He was, sir. He removed them in the back seat of the cruiser," the cop said, as he blinked nervously and his cheeks blushed with embarrassment.

After a few seconds, he looked away from his superior officer's glare. Captain Hartman looked at Gallagher suspiciously, then back at the young officer who nodded quickly and shrugged his shoulders in an "Aw, shucks" manner, providing further verification of the escape.

Gallagher watched the charade as it played out, loving every minute. Then he rubbed his wrists as if trying to stimulate the circulation with his hands and looked directly at the police captain.

"Damn cuffs—irritate the hell out of my wrists. Usually can't wait to get them off," he said.

Hartman's level of annoyance had peaked and he bellowed, "All right, wise ass, what else do I need to know about you?"

His narrowed eyes and the skeptical look on his face told Gallagher that he couldn't push this guy much further.

"My name's Gallagher. I'm a private investigator. My father-in-law had called your police station to report Kate missing but wasn't getting anywhere."

"You mean your ex-father-in-law," he said with emphasis on the "ex."

"Right," said Gallagher, not wishing to inflame Hartman's hostile attitude.

Hartman dropped a paper file onto the desk and walked around to face Gallagher.

"Well, as a private eye, you know as well as I do that when the 'ex' turns up missing, ninety per cent of the time it's the estranged husband who caused the disappearance."

"Right again."

"So that makes you the number-one suspect here."

"If that's true, why would I show up in Indiana trying to find her?"

Hartman stepped closer.

"You wouldn't be the first guy to lead the police on a wild-goose chase to cover his tracks," he said.

Hartman's garlic breath and nicotine-yellowed teeth were a potent combination.

Gallagher had no place to retreat so he exhaled slightly and replied, "True, but you're wrong about this one, Captain. I had nothing to do with Kate's disappearance. I'm trying to find her and make sure that she, her cousin, and her cousin's daughter are safe."

Hartman cast a quick glance at the suitcase. "Mind if we look in your bag?" he asked.

"Go right ahead. I've got nothing to hide."

The young officer placed the suitcase on a table, unzipped it, and began looking through the contents.

Hartman continued the questioning.

"Tell me about your ex. What brought her to visit her cousin in Indiana now?"

"Cindy's husband recently passed away. Kate came out to give her some support."

"Are they close cousins?"

"Yes. I believe they are," said Gallagher.

"But she wasn't out here for the funeral. Doesn't that strike you as being odd?"

Hartman's hostile tone added to the growing tension in the room, but his leading questions were transparent. This guy knew much more than he was letting on. Gallagher prepared himself for another shoe to drop.

"That's how they arranged it," said Gallagher, not willing to cave in to this jerk.

"Arranged?" mocked Hartman. "That's an interesting choice of words."

"Excuse me, Captain," interrupted the young officer, holding out for display a 9mm Glock automatic pistol that he had just found in Gallagher's suitcase.

Hartman looked at the gun and then made an annoyed motion to the officer to put it down on his desk.

Maybe he's afraid my Glock might go off in this kid's hand, thought Gallagher.

Hartman arched his eyebrows and flashed a harsh stare at Gallagher, "You licensed to carry?"

"Yes," said Gallagher, "The permit's in my wallet."

"You better not be lying."

Reaching into his back pocket, Gallagher removed his wallet and flipped it onto Hartman's desk.

"It's in there." Then, pointing to the young officer, Gallagher said, "Have your guy check it out."

Gallagher also thought of offering Hartman a breath mint, but feared it would only heighten the tension between them.

Hartman ignored the wallet.

"Okay, let's get back to this 'arrangement' you mentioned," he said with a sneer.

"Why don't we just cut the crap, Captain? You know all about Cindy and Kate."

Hartman nodded to Gallagher and pursed his lips, acknowledging that the man in his custody had seen through this charade. He walked slowly behind his desk and sat down. Then, he motioned to Gallagher.

"Have a seat, Gallagher. Yes, we know that Cindy and Don adopted a baby three years ago. A woman from out of town named Kathryn McSurdy delivered the baby at Lafayette General. The adoption papers were processed and certified several days later. Kathryn McSurdy flew back to Boston the next day and, according to the airline records, never returned to Indiana."

"You've got your facts in order this time, Captain," said Gallagher, interrupting Hartman's running storyline.

"Until six days ago," barked Hartman, his voice rising and refusing to allow Gallagher to interrupt any further.

The room became silent.

Both men stared at each other.

Had the air stopped moving or did the tension just ratchet up another notch? The staredown continued for a few more seconds. Gallagher began wondering where all of this would end.

Having regained his initiative, Hartman began speaking with a dramatic flare, gesturing with his index finger.

"But this is where the story gets mighty interesting," he said.

Gallagher had taken a seat and now leaned forward.

"What do you mean?"

"Cindy Kraemer, her three-year old daughter, Hayley, and your ex-wife, Kate, have not been seen or heard from by anyone for six days."

"Like I said—that's why I'm here."

"But did you know that Cindy Kraemer's burned body was recovered from her car after it had rolled off a state road, over-turned, and caught on fire?"

Gallagher sat back, shocked by this news.

His mouth dropped open.

"No," he said. "I had no idea."

Then, hesitating, almost afraid to hear the response, he asked, "Was anyone else in the car?"

"No, she was alone," said Hartman, continuing to stare at Gallagher, observing his every response.

Then he dropped the bombshell.

"But the autopsy findings were unmistakable. Cindy Kraemer had been dead a long time before someone put her in that car."

Chapter 8

Captain Hartman's news had stunned Gallagher. He sat dazed in his chair, numbed by the news of the tragic sequence of events of the past forty-eight hours.

Kate has a baby and gives it up to her cousin and her husband for adoption? Then, Don Kraemer dies from a mysterious ailment? Cindy Kraemer is murdered and then placed into a car that is set on fire?

Kate and Hayley still missing?

This is surreal!

Hartman's booming voice brought Gallagher back to reality.

"So, what's your take on all of this, Gallagher? What do you know that I should know?"

"Sorry, Captain. Wish I had something to offer," he said, shaking his head.

Then, he sat up as an important thought struck him.

"But I do have a question, Captain. What was the cause of Cindy's death?"

"Blunt-force trauma to the head. Whoever killed her hoped the car fire and explosion would cover it up. Amateur job—makes me wonder."

He paused, waiting for Gallagher to jump in.

"What are you suggesting?" asked Gallagher.

"Did your 'ex' ever express any regrets about giving up this baby?"

Gallagher shrugged.

"She never told me anything about the baby. The first I learned about it was two days ago."

"What about while you were married? Did she ever indicate that she wished she had a child?"

"No, we were preoccupied with other matters. We never really got that far. What are you driving at here?" Gallagher asked, but he had begun to sense where this discussion was headed.

Hartman stood up and began walking around his desk. He looked up toward the ceiling, apparently gathering his thoughts before expounding on a theory. Then he suddenly stopped and stared down at Gallagher. "What if Kate came out to Indiana and sees this distraught cousin who just lost her husband? Sees the baby she gave up three years ago and decides she wants her back."

Gallagher had heard enough.

"You've got to be kidding!" he said, incredulous at the suggestion. "You think Kate murdered Cindy and kidnapped Hayley? That's ridiculous! She would never do something like that. Kate would never harm anyone."

A slight smile came across Hartman's face.

This Cheshire cat look was beginning to get under Gallagher's skin.

"You Easterners think we're a bunch of country bumpkins

out here," he said. "But we do our homework. We check into a lot of things—a whole lot of things. And while we were checking her background, we discovered that your ex-wife had fired three shots into the back of an intruder about a year ago. It was ruled justifiable homicide, but a lot of questions came up. One shot should have been enough— but three? Sounds more like a person with a pretty hot temper and not hesitant to use a weapon. So don't tell me, Mr. Boston Private Investigator, that your 'ex' isn't capable of violence."

"Come on, Hartman, you can't be serious. I was the target of a hit. Two goons broke into my house and tried to kill me. Kate got home, saw what was happening, picked up a gun from the floor, and shot one of them as he was about to finish me off. Didn't you read the complete report?"

"Of course," he said, "But that doesn't change the facts we are facing here. A woman is dead; her three-year old daughter is missing; and the birth mother, who just recently arrived on the scene, is also missing. We have no other suspects and no other motives. Until we do, your ex-wife, Kate, is a person of interest in this matter. And, I might add, Gallagher, I find you to be a pretty interesting person in this case as well. You showed up right after they disappeared."

"Come on, Hartman! Knock it off! You know this is crazy."

"Maybe not," he said.

Then he warned Gallagher, "Look, you're free to go, but you better let us know where you are and what you're up to. If you hear from your ex-wife, I want her in my office for questioning. We've issued an Amber Alert for Hayley and advised that

Chapter 9

Gallagher reclaimed his suitcase, wallet, and Glock and asked for a ride back to the Kraemer home so he could pick up his rental car. Captain Hartman scoffed at the request, reminding him that the Townsend Police did not offer taxi service. Gallagher left the police station and called a local cab company from his cell phone.

Ten minutes later, a grimy white car labeled "Townsend Cab" pulled up. The windows of the cab were rolled down. The overweight driver had the seat pushed back to its limit and leaned his left arm on the door.

He gave Gallagher the once over and then asked, "You the guy who called for a cab?"

Gallagher hesitated. The cab needed a trip to the nearest car wash. A fifteen-minute vacuum job would also help. And the fact that the windows were rolled down served as a clear indication that either the AC was broken or this guy had no intention of using it.

But this was no time for nit-picking.

"Yeah, I'm the guy," said Gallagher.

"Then whattya' waitin' for? Get in," said the cabbie.

Great! Another Townsend warm and fuzzy greeting. Why does everyone I meet in this town have a problem with me? Gallagher wondered.

Despite the cabbie's initial hostility, Gallagher tried to engage him in a conversation about the Kraemers and the Amber Alert that had been issued for their daughter. At this point, even hearsay would be a good beginning. But the guy just gave him a blank look in the rearview mirror.

"Sorry, don't know nuthin' about it. How old is the girl?"

"Three."

"That's terrible," said the cab driver. "But they'll find her. That Amber Alert system works good."

Gallagher shook his head and paused for a second.

"You drive around in this cab all day, right?"

"Sure do."

"Then how come you didn't know anything about it?"

The cabbie smiled, knowing that he had just gotten bagged.

Then, with an apologetic tone, he looked at Gallagher in the rearview mirror and said, "You got a good point there. Maybe they won't find her after all."

A chilling thought for sure.

Gallagher grimaced and merely looked out the window without saying a word. *Is everyone oblivious to the search for Hayley? What's going on in this town?*

The cab arrived at 1301 Bates Avenue.

Gallagher paid the fare and asked, "Where's the nearest place for coffee?"

His addiction to the caffeinated beans still had a grip on him.

"Starbucks. Just drive down Bates to Main Street and turn left. Not even five minutes from here."

At least the cabbie was informed about something. Within a short time, Gallagher was seated at a small table sipping a twenty-ounce Venti. Black. No cream. No sugar.

He couldn't escape the thought that Kate was in serious danger. And Hayley as well.

Where should I begin? Hartman's theory about Kate is totally absurd. How do I convince the police that they're wrong? Something must have happened to Kate and Hayley. Is someone holding them against their will? The same person who killed Cindy? But why?

Gallagher looked at his watch and then out the window of the coffee shop. He was fighting against time in a strange town—a place where he had no contacts and where he couldn't count on help from the police.

Gallagher ordered another coffee and racked his brain for a plan.

Chapter 10

Gallagher found his first clue in the Townsend Public Library. He sat in the reference library section and read the obituary column of *The Lafayette Gazette* from three weeks ago. He perused the list of names until he came to the funeral notice for Donald J. Kraemer:

Donald J. Kraemer, age 45, unexpectedly, after a brief illness. Son of the late James and Jennie Kraemer. Owner of DK Landscaping, Townsend. Survived by his loving wife, Cynthia and daughter, Hayley, both of Townsend. Also survived by a brother, Norman, of West Lafayette.

Gallagher stopped reading and immediately walked over to the desk of the reference librarian. A young woman looked up and smiled.

"Excuse me, could I use one of your computers to check for a local address and phone number" he asked.

"Sure," she said, pointing over his shoulder toward a long desk with several computer stations. "You won't need a password."

Gallagher turned around, walked over to the desk and sat down in front of one of the computers. He typed in Norman

Kraemer's name and town. Then he squinted and moved closer to the screen to bring the letters into focus.

This is getting ridiculous. I've got to get a pair of reading glasses!

He found the listing he was looking for: Kraemer, Norman, 1207 Statler Road, W Laf. He scribbled the phone number and the address on a piece of scrap paper and bolted out of the library.

Maybe his brother knows something. I've got to start somewhere.

On his drive to West Lafayette, Gallagher called Kate's father. He knew he would be delivering disturbing news, but could think of no way to soften the blow.

"Hello," said Bob as he answered the phone.

"Bob, I'm in Indiana."

Bob's excited response was immediate. "Have you spoken to Kate?"

Gallagher swallowed once as he gathered his thoughts. "I wish I could say yes. But no—Kate is still missing."

"Have you talked to the police?"

"Yes, I met with a Captain from the Townsend Police earlier today. They've issued an Amber Alert for Hayley but so far there's been no response."

"An Amber Alert? I don't understand. Why isn't she with Cindy?"

"Bob, I'm afraid I have terrible news. Cindy's been murdered. Her body was recovered from a burning car a few days ago. The police are investigating but so far they have no motive—no suspects. I'm very sorry—"

"Murdered?" Bob interrupted before Gallagher could finish.

"Oh my god!" he cried, his voice growing louder in near panic.

Gallagher continued with more details. "Cindy was alone in the car. The police have no leads on Kate's whereabouts. I'm on my way to Don Kramer's brother's house. I'm hoping to get some information from him—something to go on."

"Should Barbara and I come out there? Maybe we can help."

"No, Bob. It's best for you to stay home. Take care of Barbara. Give me some time to sort this all out. I'll find them; I promise. I'll call you when I know more."

A long pause.

"Alright. I don't know how Barbara's going to take this," said Bob.

"I know. This is not easy for any of us. Try to stay calm. I'll be in touch."

"Okay."

The phone clicked.

Gallagher continued driving. A feeling of desperation had begun to take hold of him.

Chapter 11

Gallagher arrived at 1207 Statler Road within twenty minutes. He had decided not to call ahead, preferring to risk a face-to-face rebuff rather than a click and a sudden dial tone after he identified himself as a private investigator.

And imagine the response when I add that I'm the ex-husband of the woman suspected of abducting Norman Kraemer's niece?

The home was a small, one-story ranch in a neighborhood that looked like it must have been off-limits to carpenters and house painting crews.

Gallagher rang the doorbell and waited.

No response.

He rang a second time and a light went on inside the house, but still no one opened the door. Finally, after a long wait, the door slowly opened. A man in a wheelchair looked up at Gallagher. He had a stubbly beard, and his eyes were bloodshot. Gallagher wondered if he had been drinking.

"If you're selling something, I ain't buying," the man said.

His voice had an angry edge.

"Norman Kraemer?" asked Gallagher, speaking through the screen door that remained closed.

"Yeah, who's askin'?"

"My name is Gallagher. I'm a private investigator from Boston. I'm in the area trying to locate my ex-wife, Kate McSurdy. She's been reported missing by her parents and hasn't been seen or heard from in almost a week."

"Kate? You were married to Kate?"

"Yes. You've met her?"

"Yeah, right after my brother's funeral. Cindy brought her over one night with Hayley and introduced her. Her cousin from Boston! Nice woman—very nice indeed. She never mentioned bein' married."

He looked away for a second as if pondering his own question.

Then he snapped back at Gallagher, "Why'd she dump you? Were you screwin' around on her?"

"No—not at all. It's a long story."

"Usually is. I know how it goes," he said sadly and then added, "Been there myself."

Gallagher sensed a softening of Norman's initial resistance.

"Mind if I come in? I've got a lot of questions."

Norman bristled at the suggestion.

"You workin' with the police? I've told 'em everything I know, and it ain't very much. Some reporters have come around. I ain't told 'em squat. Nosy bastards! Seems like all hell's broken loose. First Don— now Cindy. And on top of that, Hayley turns up missing. That poor little angel. I don't know what to think."

Gallagher could see the pain on Norman's face.

"I'm sure this has been an awful ordeal for you. But, trust

me, I'm here to help. I'm not working with the police. In fact, they've already taken me into custody and still consider me a person of interest in this case. No, Norman, I'm just trying to get to the bottom of all of this. I need to find Kate, and while I'm at it, that includes Hayley."

Norman stared up at Gallagher, studying his unexpected visitor as if trying to determine his credibility. He reversed his wheelchair slightly to allow himself to open the main door a bit wider. Then he moved forward and unlocked the screen door.

"Come on in, Gallagher," he said. "We've got a lot to talk about."

Chapter 12

Ellie Fetterman looked up from her computer monitor and let out a gasp. She instantly recognized the imposing figure standing in the doorway of her private office at Professional Placements, Incorporated, the business she co-owned with her partner, Kate McSurdy.

"Matt!" she exclaimed, almost embarrassed by her over-reactive response. "You scared me. I wasn't expecting to see you standing there."

"I told your girl at the desk that we were old friends, and I didn't need to be announced," said Matt Winston.

He stepped into the office with a confident stride. At six feet, four inches tall and more than two hundred and fifty pounds, his swagger was a by-product of his size and years of grid-iron battles. He forced an awkward smile, but it quickly turned into a grimace.

Ellie stood up to lessen the effect of his intimidating appearance. It didn't work—he towered over her.

"What brings you here, Matt? Haven't seen you in quite a while," she said.

Her right hand reached up and nervously rubbed her cheek.

"I'm looking for Kate. I need to speak to her about a private matter."

Ellie shifted her weight uneasily. Her voice cracked, hesitating to broach the next topic.

"Now look, Matt, you know that Kate's restraining order is still in effect. You really have no business coming here."

"I'm not here to cause trouble, Ellie. I just need to talk to Kate."

"She's not here," she said.

"Where is she?" he demanded.

"I don't know. She's out of town for a while. She didn't say when she'd be back."

Ellie looked down at her phone, wondering if she needed to grab it and dial 911.

Matt's face flushed, and he moved closer.

"Where is she, Ellie? You must know when she's coming back. I'm not taking 'No' for an answer. I've got to talk to her about something important."

Now, Ellie spoke defiantly.

"Matt, if you don't leave this office immediately, I'm calling the police. I'm warning you—leave Kate alone or you'll end up in jail."

Matt stepped back and held his hands out in a peace gesture.

"All right, I'll leave. But I just have one question I want you to answer."

He paused and took a breath, gathering some control over the anger boiling within him.

"What do you know about Kate's baby—my baby?"

PULSE OF MY HEART

Ellie's brow wrinkled, and she winced.

"Baby?" she asked. Ellie shook her head in disbelief and stammered, "I—I don't know what you're talking about. I know nothing about a baby. Certainly not your baby. Where did you come up with that crazy notion?"

Matt pointed his finger at Ellie with a threatening gesture—his eyes ablaze with anger.

"You're lying to protect her. I know it! I'm going to find that child—my child! I have legal rights here, and Kate's not going to get away with this. And you can tell Kate that when you see her!"

Matt stared down at Ellie for a second, then turned, walked out of the office, and slammed the door behind him.

Shaken by the confrontation, Ellie let out a deep sigh and reached for the phone. Her hands trembled. She punched in the number of Kate's cell phone.

No one answered.

Chapter 13

Norman Kraemer pointed to a small sitting room to the right of the main entrance to the house.

"Have a seat in there," he said. "I'm comin' right behind you."

The room had a large open space next to a couch that faced a fifty-four-inch, flat-screen television. Gallagher sat down on the couch and understood the purpose of the open space when Norman drove his wheelchair into the room and parked it so he could look directly at Gallagher.

"How do you like that HDTV?" asked Norman. "Isn't that a beauty?"

"Yes, must be great for watching sports," said Gallagher.

"It was a present from my brother, Don. A man couldn't have had a better brother." Looking down at his wheelchair, Norman continued, "After my war injury forced me into this mode of transportation, he was always there for me."

His voice had a distinct tone of sadness and trailed off as he pondered his own statement.

"What happened in the war?" asked Gallagher.

"I was in infantry during the Gulf War, February of 1991,

doin' clean-up on Highway 80 comin' out of Kuwait on the way to Basra in Iraq. We were fixin' a tire on our truck when an IED exploded, and I got hit in the back with shrapnel. Severed my spinal cord. I've been paralyzed below the waist ever since."

"I'm sorry," said Gallagher. "That's a real tough break. We owe a lot to guys like you."

Norman immediately perked up as Gallagher's words seemed to have struck a nerve, but he waved his hand, dismissing the expression of gratitude.

"Thanks, if you mean that. Everybody says that same ol' bullshit—congressmen, senators, presidents: 'We owe our wounded servicemen—oh, yes, we owe our wounded servicemen.' But, in the end, guys like me are barely gettin' by. I'm sick of hearin' it."

The cause of his bitterness was now in the open.

Both men were silent. Gallagher waited, allowing Norman more time to vent. Then Norman's tone softened, and he began to reflect, as if talking to himself.

"Guess it could have been worse. If it had been a VBIED. I would have been dead."

"VBIED?" asked Gallagher.

"Vehicle Borne Improvised Explosive Device. Those are cars or trucks loaded with explosives. They're much more powerful than regular IEDs, and they spray shrapnel over a wider range. If you're standin' near one of those babies when it explodes, you usually don't live to talk about it."

Norman's war experience and personal tragedy had obviously become the all-consuming focus in his life. But Gallagher had to move the conversation along and enlist Norman's help in solving the present-day crisis.

"Norman, I understand you've gone through a lot and I wish I could listen, but we're up against time. Something's happened to Kate and Hayley, and I've got to find them before it's too late."

Norman shifted his weight to the right side of the wheelchair and leaned back.

"Tell me, Gallagher. Do you believe this police theory that Kate killed Cindy and kidnapped Hayley?"

"No. Not for a second."

Norman replied without hesitation.

"Neither do I. In fact, this whole Amber Alert is pure bullshit. I only met Kate for a short while one night, but I could tell. She wouldn't murder her cousin and abduct her child. I tried to tell that to the police when they questioned me, but they didn't want to listen."

Gallagher leaned forward to the edge of the couch.

"What happened to your brother? Kate's father told me that Cindy had been asking the police questions about Don's death."

Norman exhaled deeply and looked up at the ceiling.

"It's still so hard to believe. He was a healthy guy—jogged, worked out, did a lot of manual labor with his landscaping business. He was always very fit. But then he got a fever and began complaining of headaches. Told me he couldn't sleep at night and felt weak."

"Didn't he go to the doctor?"

"Not Don. He hated doctors. Never took medicine. Never even went for an annual physical. He just believed in eatin' right, no smokin', no drinkin', and stayin' in shape."

"But wasn't he alarmed at these sudden symptoms?" asked Gallagher.

"Sure. He thought he had come down with the flu or some sort of strange virus that would eventually run its course and go away."

"But he was wrong," said Gallagher, trying to lead Norman along and get more information.

Norman swallowed hard and shook his head.

"Yeah, I guess you could say he was dead wrong."

His eyes became misty, and he couldn't look toward Gallagher.

"Dammit, I miss him," he said as large tears began rolling down his cheeks.

Gallagher waited a few seconds, fully aware of the void that Norman felt. His thoughts immediately harkened back to his own dead brother, Tommy—killed in an automobile accident when he was just sixteen. The unspeakable sadness and total devastation at the loss of his only brother would be forever etched in Gallagher's memory.

"I'm sorry, Norman. I know this is tough for you. I lost a brother, too."

Norman sat in his wheelchair, sobbing softly, unable to respond.

Gallagher tried to convey the sense of urgency he faced.

"But Norman—the lives of two people are at stake. We

have to move on here. I need to know as much as you can tell me," he urged.

Norman pulled a tissue from his pocket and wiped his face. His stubbly beard shredded the tissue. He didn't realize that some of the tissue fragments stuck to his face. Gallagher stood up, reached over, and gently flicked the pieces of tissue away.

"Here you go, my friend. Let me help you a bit," he said.

Almost embarrassed, Norman rubbed his hand across his face to make sure all of the debris had been removed.

"Oh, thanks," he said. "You'll have to excuse me. I'm a little out of sync these days."

"Don't worry. You're doing just fine," said Gallagher.

Then, Norman seemed to gather himself and resumed talking.

"Don started actin' kind of strange. Confused. He seemed like he was hallucinatin' at times. He kept ravin' on about the Latino guy and the dog that attacked him a couple of weeks ago. But near the end, when he was in the hospital after his stroke, he wasn't makin' much sense. Then, he went into a coma and died two days later. The doctors told Cindy there was nothin' they could do for him."

"I'm so sorry for your loss, Norman. It must have been quite a shock."

"Yes, it was. Still can't believe it."

Norman sat quietly in his chair for a few seconds and then looked up at Gallagher.

"Care for a drink?" he asked.

"No thanks, Norman. I'm fine."

"Well, I need somethin'. Just a minute," he said, as he put his wheelchair into reverse, spun around, and headed toward the kitchen.

After a few minutes, he returned with a bottle of Bud Light in his hand.

"Sure you don't want a beer?" he asked.

"I'm all set, Norman. You go right ahead."

Norman leaned back and chugged a few swallows of beer from the bottle.

"Tell me about this guy and the dog. What do you know about all of that?" asked Gallagher.

Norman appeared energized by his drink and began to speak rapidly.

"Well, Don came over to visit me one afternoon. He had scratches all over his face and arms, and his right arm had a nasty set of punctures. I said, 'What the hell happened to you?' He told me he was joggin' along the Wabash Heritage Trail the day before. All of a sudden, this pit bull jumps out from the bushes, knocks him to the ground, and attacks him. He said he thought the damn dog was gonna kill him. He could barely fight the fuckin' animal off him, but then the owner showed up and pulled the dog away. The guy sounded like he had a Latino accent. He pretended to call Don's cell phone with his name and phone number and his vet's number and promised to pay for any medical bills. But, the fuckin' bastard tricked Don and never left a voicemail. The guy conned him and got away with it."

Norman threw his head back and took a few more swigs of his beer.

"So then what happened?" asked Gallagher, his interest piqued about the attack.

"Don said he was gonna report it to the police. He also wanted to know what business this guy had with an unmarked police car."

"Unmarked police car?"

"Yeah. Don said the guy ran down toward a clearing. A pickup truck was waitin' for him. He put the dog into the back of the truck and jumped into the front passenger seat. Someone else was in the driver's seat. Then, Don saw an unmarked police car drivin' away with the pickup."

"He was sure it was a police car?"

Norman took another swig from his bottle of beer and then pointed it toward Gallagher for emphasis.

"My brother knew that kind of shit. If he said it was a police car, there was no mistake about it. You could take it to the bank."

"What happened when he went to the police?"

Norman leaned forward and shook his head in disbelief.

"Don came over a few days later. He was really pissed. Said the police just totally blew him off. Wouldn't give him the time of day."

"And that was the end of it?"

"No. Don was convinced that the police were stonewallin' him. He went back with complete descriptions of the Latino guy and the dog and tried to force the police to take some action. But they basically gave him lip service and never did a thing. When Cindy came over last week, she told me that she had found some notes in Don's office at home."

"Notes? What was on them?"

"Don remembered the dog's name—Caesar—and, I guess, some other stuff. But she didn't give me any more details. Cindy was also waitin' for the laboratory findings and the results of the autopsy. Then she planned on goin' to the police herself. I could tell she was very bothered by the circumstances surroundin' Don's death, but she didn't want to talk too much about it. She said if the police didn't take any action, she was goin' to the newspapers. That night, when she was here with Kate and Hayley, was the last time I saw or heard from Cindy, so I don't know what happened."

"Any word on Cindy's funeral?"

"It's been put off for three days until the police release her body and the out-of-town family members can get here."

Gallagher had listened carefully, taking in all of the nuanced facets of Norman's story.

"Norman, can you get me into your brother's house?"

"Sure. Don and Cindy gave me a key in case of an emergency. But didn't you say the police were watchin' the house and stopped you?"

"Yes, they've got an officer parked outside to intercept any visitors."

"Then how do you plan on getting' in?"

Gallagher flashed a boyish grin and said nothing.

Chapter 14

A brisk wind blew across the lush, green pastures at Sawmill River Farm, a three-hundred acre, miniature-horse farm located ten miles northwest of Kokomo, Indiana. A sign at the entrance boasted: Championship Miniature Show Horses. One of the Finest Collections in North America. For Sale: Mares, Stallions, and Geldings.

A white fence stretched from the entrance along both sides of a one-lane road for almost a quarter of a mile leading to the main barn—a large, red building with a white roof that gleamed in the bright sunshine. A tractor connected to a flatbed trailer was parked next to the barn. A man wearing jeans and a white tee shirt was unloading bales of hay from the trailer and stacking them in a staggered, crisscross pattern. From each side of the barn, the fence extended out into a series of large, gated paddocks where dozens of miniature horses, all less than thirty-four inches tall, grazed under the watchful eye of a foreman. The stallions were isolated in their own private paddocks. When the horses ran, their perfectly groomed manes bounced up into the wind and then fell gracefully across their lower necks.

Far to the left of the barn, nearly one hundred yards away, stood a large farmhouse. Two rocking chairs, a dual-chair swing, and several high-backed wooden chairs were arranged on the front porch, which extended for the entire width of the farmhouse. The front door was closed; the shades were drawn. No other people or pets could be seen near the farmhouse.

A dirt road angled away from the rear of the farmhouse toward a densely wooded area of tall maple and birch trees. A small guest house, completely shaded by the trees and out of view from the working areas of the farm, stood at the end of the road. The building was in poor repair. In stark contrast to the other well-maintained buildings on the farm, the shabby condition of the guest house made it appear to be abandoned. The windows were boarded with plywood; a padlock secured the front door.

The inside of the guest house was sparsely furnished. The bedroom had one double bed, a closet, and a small, attached bathroom. A small sitting room had a couch, a coffee table, and a rocking chair. A refrigerator, an electric range, a sink, and a wooden table for two furnished the basic kitchen.

A little girl looked up at a woman sitting next to her on the couch.

"Aunt Kate, read me another book," she said.

"Of course, sweetheart," said Kate.

She lifted the little girl onto her lap and kissed her tenderly on the cheek.

"Which book would you like to read this time?" she asked, reaching for the stack of four children's books on the coffee table.

Her hands trembled as she tried to hold the books while the little girl made her selection. The trembling alone was normally enough to set off another emotional outburst, but Kate wouldn't allow it.

No, I've got to remain strong; I've got to keep myself together for Hayley's sake.

Kate McSurdy, held captive for days with no apparent chance for escape and fearing for Hayley's safety, fought back tears and desperately tried to maintain her composure.

Her thoughts were consumed with one tormenting question: *Will we ever get out of here alive?*

Chapter 15

A silver Dodge Grand Caravan pulled up to the curb in front of 1301 Bates Avenue in Townsend. The automatic kneeling system lowered the van closer to the ground. The sliding door opened toward the rear, and a motorized wheelchair ramp extended out toward the sidewalk. Norman Kraemer drove his wheelchair across the ramp and onto the incline of the handicapped accessible sidewalk.

Thoughts of his brother, Don, flashed through his mind. He vividly remembered how Don had petitioned the Department of Public Works to modify the curb and install a handicapped-accessible ramp on the sidewalk in front of his house because of the frequent visits of his brother, Norman, a disabled veteran of the Gulf War. It had taken months and several appearances before the Town Board in order to secure approval for the work.

Persistence. One of Don's outstanding characteristics.

But, in the end, he had prevailed and the Board had approved the project. Don had always done everything to make Norman's life easier.

God, I miss him, thought Norman.

Norman made his way down the sidewalk, then up the

driveway toward the ramp leading up to the front door of the house.

The door of a police cruiser parked on Atwood Street opened, and a police officer stepped out.

"Hey!" he shouted. "Hold it right there!"

Norman ignored the request and kept motoring toward the front door.

Now in a near sprint across the lawn, the police officer shouted again, "Hey! I said stop right there!"

Norman looked to his right at the approaching police officer. His wheelchair suddenly veered to the edge of the ramp and then careened off balance, toppling over onto the lawn.

Norman spilled out of his wheelchair, sprawled on the lawn, and began screaming, "Aaagh! My back! Oh, my God!—my back!"

He twisted and contorted his body violently as he tried to reach behind to his lower back with his left arm

The panicked police officer rushed to his side.

"Don't move, sir. Try to stay calm. Let me call for help." He spoke frantically into his shoulder mic, "Emergency at 1301 Bates Avenue. Disabled man seriously injured. Request immediate assistance."

Norman continued to writhe on the ground in obvious pain.

"What the hell is wrong with you?" he yelled. "You scared the shit out of me and made me fall! Aagh!" he groaned, as he reached for his back.

Then his eyes narrowed and he gritted his teeth.

"You're gonna pay for this, you stupid bastard! This is my

brother's house. Why the hell are you hasslin' me?"

The officer ignored Norman's rant and placed one hand on Norman's shoulder and the other on his hip trying to stabilize him and prevent any further movements.

"Try to stay still, sir," he said. "Help is on the way."

Norman's agonizing groans persisted as he buried his face in the grass and clutched aimlessly at his back.

"Damn cops! Damn cops! This is your fuckin' fault," he cried.

The bewildered young officer looked around nervously and then back at Norman, almost begging for assistance.

As he lay on the ground, Norman wondered if he had given Gallagher enough time to find what he was looking for.

Chapter 16

Matt Winston studied the laminated sign on the door: "Joel Braxton: Private Investigator." He turned the knob, opened the door, and walked in. The reception room was small—hardly impressive: two stack chairs, a table with a few wrinkled magazines scattered on the top, and a wooden coat rack full of nicks and scratches.

Furnished by Home Depot or Building 19 1/2? This guy is supposed to be one of the best private eyes in Boston. How come this place is such a dump?

Matt shook his head and gave a slight shrug as he sat down on one of the plastic stack chairs.

The door to the rear office was slightly ajar and a voice called out, "Mr. Winston? You're right on time."

The door swung open and a short, balding man appeared at the entrance.

"Come on in," he said.

Matt stood up and walked toward the man, who extended his hand and said, "Joel Braxton—pleased to meet you." Then he exclaimed, "My word! You are a big guy, aren't you? I could use someone your size for protection."

"Matt Winston," Matt said, shaking Braxton's hand politely but giving him a skeptical look as he towered over the smaller man. "If you're a private eye, you carry a gun. Right? Why would you need me for protection?"

Braxton laughed at the quick comeback. As they walked into the rear office, he made a big wave with his left arm and motioned to Matt to sit down on a chair in front of his desk.

"I'm more of a research investigator. I never carry a weapon. Maybe I should," he cracked. "Occasionally I dig up things that make some folks pretty angry."

"That's why I was referred to you. I hear you're pretty good at uncovering facts that people don't want to reveal. These days it seems like everyone's hiding behind the privacy laws."

"Well, the privacy laws are certainly obstacles we have to contend with," Braxton said.

Then he smiled slyly.

"But there are ways to get around them."

"In my case," Matt said, "I feel like I've got a right to certain information that directly affects me. And so far, no one has been willing to give it to me. I'm up against a brick wall."

"Okay," said Braxton, slapping his desk as he leaned back in his chair. "I guess we're past the introductions. You've come to the right place. No more bullshitting around. What do you need to know?"

Matt didn't hesitate.

"I was in a relationship with a woman for almost four years. When we broke up, she was pregnant, but she never told me. I believe she had the baby out of state—might have put it up for adoption. I want to know what happened. If there's a child—if my child is alive somewhere, I want to know."

Braxton dropped his jovial tone and sat forward, placing his hands together and both elbows on his desk.

"You're not alone here. This is a common problem. But it usually involves an expensive search and then a lengthy legal battle to establish paternity. You need blood tests—maybe even a DNA lab and expert. Are you prepared for all of that?"

"Whatever it takes," said Matt solemnly.

He gave a serious stare at Braxton to verify his commitment.

Braxton's face also assumed a serious look. Without a hint of emotion, he spouted his business terms in a mechanical cadence.

"I'll need a two-thousand-dollar retainer to start. My hourly rate is two hundred and fifty. Travel and expenses are extra. And so are any payoffs to informants. In an investigation of this nature, I may have to grease a palm or two to get privileged information. I give no guarantees that I'll find what you're looking for. When we reach five-thousand-dollars in billable hours or other expenses, we'll get together and see if you want to continue."

Then, he gave Matt a wry, cocky smile.

"But, Mr. Winston, I can assure you. I usually get results. My clients are rarely dissatisfied."

Matt's mouth opened slightly, taken aback by the frank and business-like nature of Braxton's presentation. He cleared his throat, swallowed once, and nodded in acknowledgment of the terms that had been outlined. Knowing that the upfront money was required before they went any further, he reached into his jacket and brought out a pen and his checkbook.

As Matt began writing out a deposit check, Braxton continued with his poker-faced instructions.

"I'll need names, dates, and as much background history as possible."

Matt looked at Braxton who was now ready with pen in hand and a lined, yellow notepad in front of him.

"Her name at the time we were together was Kathryn McSurdy," said Matt.

Then, he furrowed his brow and paused, appearing to reconsider his statement.

"But no one ever calls her Kathryn; she always goes by Kate."

Braxton jotted the name on his notepad and gave no response.

Matt continued, "The baby would be about three years old."

Braxton looked up.

"You realize, of course, that she could have had an abortion. I may find out that there is no child."

"I know—but I doubt that she would do that."

Braxton curled his lip and nodded.

"Alright—what else?"

"I've tried to reach Kate, but I can't get in touch with her. No one will tell me where she is."

"Did she move out of town?'

"Not as far as I know. I think she's been in Boston ever since we broke up."

"Do you have a picture of her?"

"Probably at my apartment. I'll get it to you."

"Anything else I need to know?"

"About a year ago, she married a private investigator—a guy named Gallagher. Don't know if she took his name or not. From what I've been told, the marriage didn't last too long. Heard they got divorced."

Now it was Braxton's turn to look surprised.

"Gallagher? Did you say a private eye named Gallagher?"

"Yeah—you know him?"

Braxton paused. He raised his eyebrows.

"Unfortunately, the answer is yes. We're not exactly the best of friends."

He got up and walked away from his desk.

He shook his head and then added, "Gallagher and I have had our share of run-ins over the years."

"What kind of run-ins?"

Braxton gave a dismissive wave of his hand while still pacing around the room.

"Oh, nothing big—nothing to worry about. Let's just say we've had some professional disagreements," he said with a pompous tone. "We have different ideas about how to conduct a private investigation. But I won't let my relationship with Gallagher affect your case."

Then Braxton asked, "Ever meet him?"

Matt shook his head, "No, never did. Actually, I looked him up online and went to his office yesterday to see if he might be able to tell me something about Kate. But he wasn't in, and his secretary sort of blew me off. Wouldn't give me the time of day. Seems like a pattern here. When I went to Kate's office, her business partner clammed up, too. She wouldn't tell me a thing about Kate's whereabouts. It seems like she's gone into hiding or something."

Braxton scratched at his forehead.

"Did you tell Gallagher's secretary what this was all about?"

"No. Figured I shouldn't say anything unless I could talk directly to him."

"Good. Let's try to keep him out of this for as long as possible."

Matt seemed puzzled by Braxton's reaction. He waited a second and then added a little more to his background story.

"You know, I was persona non grata to Kate after we broke up."

Braxton forced a laugh.

"Let me guess—that means she has a restraining order against you. What happened, Matt—did you get a bit physical with her?"

Matt blinked a few times and winced. Braxton had struck a nerve.

"She made a big deal out of nothing! I hardly hit her. That restraining order really wasn't fair. That judge had no right …" Matt started, his voice rising with anger.

"Save it, Matt," said Braxton, trying to cool down his excitable new client.

He squinted and eyed Matt curiously, taken aback by the emotional outburst.

"Remember—I'm on your side," he said. "A lot happens when a couple splits."

Braxton continued walking around in a small semicircle at the side of his desk. He rubbed his chin a few times. The private eye seemed itchy all of a sudden.

Then, he asked, "Do you think Gallagher knows that Kate had your baby?"

"I have no idea," Matt said.

He took a deep breath.

"But what does that matter?" he asked.

Braxton hesitated, still deep in thought. He crossed his arms and continued his methodical pacing.

"I find it fascinating that I'm going to investigate the pregnancy of Gallagher's former wife, a woman who suddenly seems to have made herself hard to find. I wonder how Gallagher fits in here? One thing I do know about him— he doesn't like it when somebody butts into his personal life. He was pretty upset about the media coverage of that well-publicized dust-up he had about a year ago."

"Dust-up?"

"Oh, yeah. Didn't you see it in the newspapers?"

"I don't read the newspapers very much. Maybe I was out of town. What happened?"

"Gallagher gets himself involved in some pretty deep shit. A couple of guys tried to rub him out. If I remember correctly, his wife came along, picked up a gun and shot one of the guys to help Gallagher get out of it. I guess that would have been Kate."

Matt shook his head in disbelief.

"Yes, it must have been Kate. I had no idea. I can't believe I didn't hear about this. How did it all work out?" he asked.

Braxton shrugged his shoulders.

"It got washed away. No charges. But I heard that Gallagher gave some of the reporters a hard time. Like I said, he takes these things personal."

Matt stiffened. Braxton's words had triggered another reaction. Matt's voice exploded in anger.

"But this baby doesn't involve him! It's between me and Kate—no one else!" he said in a voice rising in anger.

Braxton gave a sarcastic smirk.

"Trust me on this one, Matt. Before we get to the bottom of all of this—before we find Kate and your missing child—we'll have to deal with Gallagher. One way or the other, we'll have to deal with Gallagher."

Chapter 17

Gallagher unlocked the rear door of Cindy and Don's house and slipped in quietly. He could hear voices coming from the front yard, especially the penetrating sound of Norman's guttural groans and tirades against the detail cop.

Good ol' Norman. Playin' him like a fiddle.

Gallagher had a self-imposed time limit on this search. Five minutes maximum before the EMTs and police backup would arrive. So, he quickly made his way through the small mud room and down the hallway. As he passed the kitchen, he noticed the sink—filled with dirty glasses, dishes, and silverware.

No one going on a trip would leave a mess like this.

Something must have happened after dinner before Kate and Cindy had a chance to clean up.

But what?

He walked into the living room. A "Goodnight Moon" game playing board and matching cards were scattered around the couch and on the floor. He saw a throw pillow from the couch under the glass coffee table. A child's plastic cup was turned on its side on top of the table, with the dried residue of orange juice surrounding the cup.

He backed out of the living room, still sizing up the scene of disarray. Then, he turned down the hallway leading to the bedrooms. A quick glance into the small study adjacent to the living room revealed another cluttered mess. The drawers to the desk were haphazardly opened; papers were strewn all over the desk and floor.

The room appeared ransacked.

Gallagher wasted no time here. Whoever preceded him had already found whatever of importance this room contained.

Several steps further down the hallway, and a look into the master bedroom yielded nothing—the bed was made; the room was neat; nothing out of place. Even the brightly decorated child's bedroom with an antique, white-brass bed looked undisturbed. Not even a toy on the floor.

Gallagher walked into the guest bedroom.

His heart sank.

A dark-green, overnight travel suitcase on wheels stood in the corner near the foot of the bed. A gold ribbon dangled from the handle—the owner's attempt to distinguish it from other bags that came off an airport luggage carousel.

Gallagher recognized it immediately as Kate's suitcase.

Somehow this inanimate object—a simple suitcase—served as a chilling reminder that Kate had left this house unexpectedly, without her belongings and the careful preparation and planning that the police had insinuated. On the contrary, it was likely that her departure had been sudden.

Had she been forcefully abducted?

Were Hayley and Cindy with her when someone barged in?

Now Cindy is dead. My god! How did all of this happen?

Who the hell did this?

Wild scenarios raced through his mind as his eyes darted around the room looking for answers. He found none. All he could find were Kate's clothes—hanging still in the small closet. He resisted the urge to reach out and touch them.

Norman's droning voice from the front of the house penetrated the walls, reassuring Gallagher that the attention of the cop remained fully occupied. But not for much longer; surely by now an ambulance had been dispatched. Gallagher had no time to waste.

His heart beat quickened.

He stepped back into the hallway and looked briefly to his right into the bathroom shared by Hayley's room and the guest bedroom. He resumed walking. Then, he stopped abruptly and turned around. Something on the floor had caught his eye.

A shiny object.

Did it belong to Kate?

He pushed the bathroom door open a little wider, walked in, and looked down at a thin pencil lying on the floor between the sink and the toilet. The label read: "L'Oreal Paris, Brown 797, Extra-Intense."

Kate's eyeliner.

Kate had always been meticulous about putting her makeup and personal items away neatly in a zippered bag.

Left on the floor? Never.

He crouched down to pick up the eyeliner pencil. He started to get up and then stopped midway and crouched down again to study a mark on the white tile floor. The pencil had been carefully placed to cover a small arrow drawn on the tile. The arrow pointed to the right—toward the wall and its window. Gallagher looked at the wall around the window hoping for another clue.

Nothing out of the ordinary.

The blinds were partially closed; the window locked.

He saw no signs or words to guide him and no other markings.

He bent down again and studied the floor, looking for something he might have missed, but he found nothing.

That arrow must be there for a reason!

The need to carefully study the area conflicted with the urgency to get out of the house before he was caught by the police.

Gallagher's pulse pounded.

He looked again at the arrow and the floor all around it. The arrow simply pointed to the right. But there was nothing to see. What was he missing? Then he smiled. The purpose of Kate's arrow had suddenly become perfectly clear.

Of course, a message left in a place where someone quickly inspecting this bathroom would never look.

He lifted the toilet seat.

He stopped before his hand brought the seat to rest against the tank. The letters "SRF" were scribbled with the eyeliner pencil on the underside of the toilet seat.

SRF? Someone's initials? Or a location?

The sound of sirens approached. Gallagher shoved the

pencil into his pocket and grabbed a tissue from the counter. He rubbed the initials off the underside of the seat and then the arrow from the floor. He walked out of the bathroom and swiftly down the hallway. He left the house through the rear door, closing and locking it carefully as he made his exit.

Gallagher looked back over his shoulder. He could see the flashing lights of emergency vehicles in front of the house as he slipped off into the woods undetected.

Chapter 18

Gar Kearney's phone had been ringing all morning. As the chief investigative reporter for the *Lafayette Eagle-Tribune*, his story in this morning's edition had stirred up a firestorm of gossip and speculation. The headline had read: "Mystery Surrounds Disappearance of Child Named in Recent Amber Alert." As usual, Gar had done a thorough job of verifying the background and details for his story. He had also relied on his inside, unnamed sources at the police department who consistently leaked information to him about ongoing investigations.

A veteran of the newspaper business, Gar nevertheless enjoyed the excitement of breaking a major story, and this story was the type that really sold newspapers.

It had all the elements of tragedy and gossip that the public loved to devour: a missing child whose parents had died mysteriously during the past few weeks and the mother's out-of-town cousin, who turned out to be the missing child's natural mother and who now had also disappeared.

Gar knew that most of the calls he received today would be from crack-pots and conspiracy mongers with wild theories about Hayley Kraemer's disappearance and her possible location. But he took the calls anyway. Once in a while, one of these nutcakes came up with an idea that made some sense and provided a critical clue that helped solve the case. Gar had also found that his readers were more likely to call him than contact the police. The police intimidation factor scared many people away. And what if the police traced the call and tried to link the caller to the crime because of information they possessed? For most folks, the answer was, "No, thanks."

A newspaper reporter was a much safer choice for the person who wanted to air a hunch, report a sighting, or simply drop a dime. Besides, the possibility of receiving credit in the newspaper as a contributing source and a good citizen was a lure that most readers couldn't resist.

Gar sat at his desk with the blinking lights of four phone lines while he took one call after another. The steady stream of calls had gone on unabated for nearly an hour. The long hold time had hardly been a deterrent. He finished one call and pressed the next blinking button.

"Gar Kearney," he said.

"Mr. Kearney," the caller said. "I read your columns all the time. They're great. Hey, I just wanna' say that woman ran off with that little girl," the man screeched.

"A lot of people feel that way," Gar said.

He looked up at the ceiling, knowing this guy sounded like a buffoon.

"But what makes you come to that conclusion, sir? Do you know something that supports your theory?" he asked.

Silence.

Then a click.

The caller was gone.

Gar shook his head.

Idiot!

He took a sip from his coffee and pressed another blinking button.

"Gar Kearney," he said.

"Mr. Kearney," the caller said. "I read your column this morning and have some questions about this case. Any chance I could stop by to see you today?"

The caller had a smooth, educated voice.

Gar leaned back in his chair.

"I'm pretty swamped today, but that's always a possibility. It depends upon what type of information you have to offer. Who's calling?" he asked.

"My name's Gallagher. I'm a private investigator."

A long pause.

Then a question.

"Are you a local guy? Don't think I've heard your name before. I know most of the private eyes in this area."

"No. I'm from Boston."

"And this case brought you all the way to Indiana?"

"Yes. I have a personal interest in it."

"How so? Did someone hire you to investigate this little girl's disappearance?"

"No, I wasn't hired. I was married to her birth mother. Kathryn McSurdy is my former wife."

Gar hesitated, taken aback by Gallagher's statement.

What a break! he thought. *Another juicy ingredient to add to the next installment of this story.*

He looked at his watch.

"Actually, I've got an opening in my schedule. I can see you today. Are you free now?

"Yes."

"How 'bout if we meet for coffee and a quick bite?"

"Sounds good to me. Just name where."

"Java Roaster on North Third Street. Do you know the place?"

"I'll find it. See you there in half an hour," said Gallagher.

The phone clicked.

Gar looked down at the blinking lights on his phone. He felt no need to take any more calls. He pressed the intercom for the newsroom switchboard.

"Marie, I've got to run to an appointment. Send the rest of my calls to voicemail. I'll be back in a couple of hours."

Chapter 19

Within twenty-five minutes, Gallagher walked into Java Roaster, a casual coffeehouse in the downtown district. The place was busy with a noisy morning crowd. He stopped by the counter and looked around.

A voice bellowed from the second level, "Gallagher?"

He looked up at a white-haired man leaning over the railing with his finger extended, pointing at him. The man waved.

Gallagher nodded and walked up the stairs.

Gar Kearney had already secured a table for two that had a large cup of coffee in front of each chair. A muffin—minus one bite—rested next to one of the coffees. Kearney motioned to the chair near the single coffee.

"It's a dark roast—their best blend. Take anything with it?"

"Dark roast is fine. I take it black."

"Something to eat?"

"The coffee's enough, thanks," said Gallagher.

He sat down and pulled the wooden chair forward. He looked across at Kearney—a man in his mid-sixties with a friendly face. He wore rimless glasses and had a thick white mustache that hung down, completely covering his upper lip.

His long white hair was thin on the top of his head and swept backward on the sides. If he grew a beard and put on thirty pounds, he'd make a great Santa Claus.

Kearney reached over to shake Gallagher's hand.

"Gar Kearney. Pleased to meet you. I'm interested in what you have to say about the Hayley Kraemer case," he said.

Gallagher returned the handshake and slid his business card across the table.

"I read your story—in fact, I read it twice just to make sure I hadn't missed anything. You covered a lot of ground and raised some wild possibilities, including one that Kate may have kidnapped Hayley. I'm telling you right now— there's no way that happened."

Kearney nodded and half-smiled in agreement.

"Gallagher, I've been an investigative reporter for a long time now, so I never rule anything out. I've been shocked to find out that some wild possibilities—things that I never gave a chance of being true that turned out to be just that— true as could be. But, in this case—no. I agree with you. I don't think your ex-wife kidnapped Hayley Kraemer."

Gallagher's eyes narrowed as he stared across at Kearney.

"So, what do you think happened?"

"I believe they were both abducted. I can't tell you why or by whom, but I do think that whoever killed Cindy Kraemer knows the answers to those questions."

Gallagher waited to see if Kearney had anything more to offer. He took a slow sip from his coffee.

After a few seconds of silence, he asked, "Are we off the

record here?"

"Absolutely. I have never revealed my sources."

"I mean off the record so that nothing we discuss or discover gets published until I say it's alright."

"You've got my word on it."

They made eye contact.

Neither man blinked.

Gallagher nodded.

A deal had been struck.

"What do you know about Don Kraemer's death?" Gallagher asked.

Kearney looked confused. He shrugged and pushed his lower lip forward.

"Nothing less than it was a real-life tragedy. A young, healthy man with a successful business and a happy family life—suffers a massive stroke and dies at the hospital a couple of days after being admitted. End of story."

"I think there's much more to his death than that. I believe he contracted rabies from an attack by a dog. Rabies led to rapid neurological degeneration, then to his stroke, and his ultimate death."

Kearney's mouth dropped open slightly and he raised an eyebrow.

"Rabies? No one ever suggested that. Can you prove this?"

"I intend to. It should be on the autopsy report. The doctors at the hospital probably missed it at first. Easy for that to happen because Don ignored all the early signs and refused to go to a doctor until it was too late."

Kearney frowned. He looked even more confused

"But what's the relevance here? It's still the same story-line—young man dies and leaves a wife and a three-year-old little girl."

"No. That's the simple version they'd like you to buy. Don Kraemer was attacked by a dog while he was out jogging along the Wabash Heritage Trail. The owner of the dog concealed his true identity and gave Don a bogus name and address. Don began to realize that he had stumbled upon some kind of deal that was going down. When he followed up with the police, they stonewalled him."

Now it was Kearney's turn to listen intently. Gallagher didn't let him ponder this new information for very long.

"Tell me about the local police, Gar. Which departments use unmarked cars?"

"Hmmm—" Kearney paused while thinking.

"Well, the town police don't really have any. All of their cars are marked. But the county police—the sheriff's department. They've got some unmarked cars. I've seen them."

Gar thought for a second, shook his head again, and then raised his hands off the table, asking for more details.

"But what's the significance of an unmarked police car?"

"An unmarked police car was present at the site where I believe this deal happened. Don saw it driving away after he was bitten by the dog."

"How'd you come up with all of this?"

"Same way you do, Gar. I ask a lot of questions."

Kearney had no response. He took another large bite from

his muffin and wiped the crumbs off his mustache. He looked around the coffee shop at the other patrons. His well-informed inquisitor had taken him by surprise. Kearney tapped the fingers of his right hand on the table as he appeared to be sorting out these new angles to the case.

"What's the jurisdiction of the sheriff's department in Indiana?" Gallagher asked.

Gar stopped the finger tapping and shrugged.

"Pretty much the same as in other states. The local cops handle anything within the town limits. The sheriff handles the county—the county and state roads and all the little townships that don't have their own police forces. They also run the county jail and the transport of prisoners. And they take care of the issues with drug busts, drug trafficking, and illegal guns."

"Do you have a contact in the sheriff's office? Someone I can talk to; someone you trust?"

Kearney pushed the last piece of the muffin into his mouth.

Still chewing, he responded, "They're not crazy about reporters over there. I'll try to put in a call a little later."

Gallagher looked at his watch.

"We're up against the clock here, Gar. We don't have any time to waste."

Kearney shot a glare at Gallagher. Gallagher's impatience and aggressiveness irritated him slightly, but he had read Gallagher's state of mind.

"Alright—alright," he said. "It's noisy in here, but I'll give the office a call right now."

Kearney looked down through his bifocals and scrolled

through the contact list of his cell phone. He stopped, punched the number on his keypad and held his phone close to his left ear.

"Don't give him too many details," said Gallagher.

Kearney moved the phone away from his mouth.

"I know—just the basics. Don't worry," he retorted.

His annoyance level rose with each of Gallagher's comments. Someone answered.

"Hey, it's Gar Kearney from the Lafayette Eagle Tribune."

After a few seconds Kearney perked up.

"Oh, yes, Deputy Norris. Thanks for remembering me. Hey, I'm sitting in Java Roaster with a private detective from Boston. He's in town investigating the Hayley Kraemer disappearance—you know the Amber Alert that was activated yesterday. His name is Gallagher. Seems like a good guy. Any chance you or one of the other deputies can spare a few minutes and talk to him? He may be able to shed some light on your case."

Gar held the phone away from his mouth and listened. Then he winked and nodded toward Gallagher.

"Yeah, I think he can make it over to your office in an hour."

He lifted his chin and raised his eyebrows, seeking a response from Gallagher. Gallagher looked at his watch again and then gave a thumbs up.

"Yes. He'll be there in an hour. Thanks for the favor."

Kearney punched the "end" button and placed his phone on the table. He gave Gallagher a deadpan look. He waited a few seconds. The ball was back in Gallagher's court.

"Thanks, Gar," said Gallagher. "I'll need directions."

"No problem. Just see the Deputy Norris at the main desk. He'll take care of you. What else?" he asked, as took a notepad from his pocket and began jotting out the directions.

"If you had a sick dog, where would you take it?"

Kearney stopped and gave an exasperated shrug. "Jeez, there are loads of vets around Lafayette. I don't…"

Gallagher interrupted, "No, I mean *really* sick. An animal hospital or a place with an emergency room for animals. I'd like to find the owner of that dog."

"Well, that would have to be Clarkson Animal Hospital in West Lafayette. Not far off the Interstate. It's the only animal hospital in the area. They've got a vet available 24/7. Someone looking for an emergency room for their pet would probably go there."

"One final question," said Gallagher. "Do the initials SRF mean anything to you?"

"S—R—F," he said, repeating the letters slowly to make sure they registered.

Kearney looked away and then shook his head.

"No, no one's initials that I can think of."

"How about an abbreviation for a place—somewhere around this area?"

Kearney thought for a few seconds more. Then his eyes widened as an idea popped into his head.

"Well, Cindy Kraemer's burned car and her body were found on Willard Road. That's just off State Road 5. Could that be it?"

Gallagher took a deep breath.

"State Road 5? It's possible, but I doubt it. Why not just write the number '5' instead of the letter 'F'?" he asked, directing the question to himself rather than Kearney.

Gallagher looked away, apparently stumped and unable to come up with an answer.

Kearney delayed jumping back into the conversation right away so as not to disturb Gallagher's thoughts.

Finally, he said, "Sorry, if that's not it, I can't help you there."

He ripped the top sheet off his notepad and slid it over to Gallagher. Then, he jotted the initials down and slipped the notepad back into his pocket.

"I'll keep them in mind and let you know if I come up with anything. What's the significance? Where'd you find them?"

Gallagher looked across at Gar Kearney. He liked this guy and hated to be evasive. After all, he had gone out of his way to help and seemed to have solid connections in this town. So Gallagher gave an answer that was sure to get Kearney's attention and keep him focused on the search for more clues.

"I don't want to overstate this, Gar. Let's just say that those initials are probably the key to finding Kate and Hayley alive."

Chapter 20

One night earlier

Her usual nighttime routine was completed. First, she read a storybook to Hayley. Then, when Hayley started to tire, Kate rubbed her back gently until the little girl fell asleep. As with most nights, Hayley was asleep by nine o'clock and would sleep soundly until at least eight the next morning.

The evening hours alone were maddening for Kate. The only sound that penetrated the walls of the small cabin was the symphony of grinding and chirping from cicadas and crickets that inhabited the surrounding woods. The fact that the cabin was located in a densely wooded area, far removed from a busy road, was merely an assumption made by Kate based on the sounds she heard each night.

Never cars or trucks.

No horns blowing or tires screeching.

No voices or music.

Only the sounds of nature.

The silence of isolation had become frightening. There were moments when she shivered with fear.

At times, she found herself begging for the sound of a siren—a police car or an ambulance. Someone to come to their rescue and return them to a safe place—away from these dangerous and desperate men, who she feared would change their minds and decide to leave no living witnesses to their crime.

At other times, she agonized over the night these men had stormed through the back door of Cindy's house. Cindy had left the house earlier—hell-bent on a mission. The inaction of the police since Don's death had frustrated and angered her. Cindy had received a copy of Don's autopsy report from the hospital. Now, finally, she had the proof she needed. She had decided to confront the police and force them to begin an investigation. If the police wouldn't cooperate, she'd go to the newspapers. She had asked Kate to watch Hayley while she drove to the police station with the report. She had made a call, and then had left the house.

Kate and Hayley had waited.

But Cindy had never returned.

In her haste to leave the house, Cindy had forgotten to lock the back door—a seemingly small mistake but one that became catastrophic.

When the break-in started, if she'd had a few seconds more Kate could have pressed 911 on her phone and called the police for help. But the men had been quick. They had burst through the door, surprised to find someone home.

Kate had no time to react.

She had been overwhelmed, then restrained by three men—three desperate men.

The leader had warned Kate to be quiet or the little girl would be hurt. Fearing for Hayley's safety, she had no other options but to cooperate. She had cradled Hayley close to her body and had tried to calm her as the men ransacked the study, looking for something. Kate never knew what they had been searching for or whether they had found it.

What was their purpose?

During those few terrorizing minutes, the leader had approached her. He had reached out and grabbed her head tightly. Again, he had issued his threat. No screams or calls for help. No harm would come to Hayley if Kate did not resist.

Then, he had explained that a hood would be placed over Kate's head. She and the girl would be taken away to another place where they would be safe and ultimately released.

But Hayley had become hysterical—fearing these threatening strangers. She had begged to use the bathroom. Kate had sworn to cooperate and had pleaded to be allowed to take her—to calm her down before they left.

The leader had relented. While the other men continued to rummage through drawers and papers in the study, he had checked the bathroom to ensure that it had no telephone that could be used to call for help. Then he had allowed Kate and Hayley to enter.

Kate had demanded privacy.

Thank god he had allowed it.

She had closed the door.

Kate had little time to act but had to do something—leave a sign or a clue to help the police. But what? And where?

Panic had begun to overcome her. This man would surely check the room.

I've got to do something. I need a place where this man will not see it!

Her only thought was about when he had reached out and he had turned to the side—she had seen the insignia on the sleeve of his shirt. She couldn't make out the words. Just the initials above them: SRF. Nothing else. She had no time to write any other words or message of her own.

Just those initials.

Would they mean something to someone? Kate prayed every night that the answer would be "yes."

She struggled to fall sleep. But her efforts were useless.

They were isolated and alone in this cabin—held captive for six days and too afraid to risk an escape.

It was a nightmare with no end in sight.

She felt a chill as she stared up at the ceiling.

For Kate, the nights were the most frightening times of all.

Will we ever get out of this place alive?

Chapter 21

11:00 am

Gallagher walked briskly to his car following his meeting with Gar Kearney. His stride lengthened. His steps were now more than hurried. He glanced at his watch again.

He had become consumed with time. The minutes and seconds kept ticking in his head.

Are they ticking away the lives of Kate and Hayley?

Gallagher started the engine and drove off. He squinted at the small notepaper on which Gar had scribbled the directions: "Head west toward Interstate—10 miles to State Road 38. Exit right—go ¼ mile past strip mall—sheriff's barracks on left—About 40 minutes from here."

Gallagher tried to dart around the traffic and beat the stop lights.

His cell phone rang. Diane's voice came from the speaker phone.

"Dan, I thought you should know—a man stopped by the office looking for you. Matt Winston. Do you know him?"

Gallagher paused. The tightness in his chest ratcheted up another notch.

"Not really. We never met, but I know a lot about him. Kate lived with him before I met her. What made him show up all of a sudden?"

"I don't know but he was very pushy. He's an intimidating type. He wanted to know where he could find you and said it was urgent, but I didn't tell him anything."

Gallagher's mind began swirling.

Matt Winston?

Everything Gallagher ever heard about the guy was bad. Kate had a restraining order against him. Her father had wanted to kill him for abusing Kate.

Now, Kate and Hayley are missing, and this guy calls out of the blue?

Could he possibly have a part in this?

"Are you still there?" asked Diane.

"Yes, sorry. I was just thinking about a few things. Did he give you any idea what it was about?"

"No, he wouldn't say. He gave me his number and said you should call him ASAP."

"Alright. I'm driving now. Text the number to me, and I'll call him as soon as I can."

"Any news on Kate?" she asked. "I'm so worried about her."

"So am I. But so far, I don't have much to go on."

"You'll find her. I know it."

"We need a break soon or it'll be too late. I'm on my way to the sheriff's office. Maybe they've got something."

"Good luck. Call me if you need anything. I'll send that number."

Within a few seconds, Gallagher's cell phone chimed. The text message appeared on the screen.

He pulled over to the side of the road and left the motor running.

He turned on the flashing hazard lights.

Then he pressed the phone number into the keypad and waited for Matt Winston to answer.

Chapter 22

"Mr. Kraemer, are you sure you want to be discharged?" asked the young doctor in the emergency room at Lafayette General Hospital.

"Yeah, I wanna' get out of here and go home," Norman pleaded. "I think it was just a back spasm."

"Is there someone at home to help you?"

"No, I live alone. But I know how to take care of myself after all this time. I'll be alright."

"But you arrived here in an ambulance complaining of severe pain," the doctor said. His skepticism was out in the open.

"I know, Doc. But I've been through this before. These spasms seem to come and go—especially if I take a fall. If it weren't for that stupid cop, this never would have happened in the first place. My x-rays were okay, weren't they?"

"Yes, there's no new structural damage that we can see. But we'll need an MRI to confirm that."

"Nah, I don't want no MRI. No more x-rays. Just get me outta' here and tell the fuckin' police to leave me alone," he demanded.

"Calm down, Mr. Kraemer. I'm a doctor; I have no control

over the police. You'll have to sign a waiver that says you are requesting a discharge against my recommendations."

"I'll sign whatever you want. I just wanna' go home."

Norman reached over to the table on the side of his bed and grabbed a plastic cup filled with water.

"See this, Doc? I can move around pretty good now. No problem."

"Okay, Mr. Kraemer. It's your choice. I'll have the nursing supervisor prepare your discharge papers."

The doctor turned and walked toward the door.

"Oh, Doc," Norman said. "Do you think someone could give me a lift to my brother's house? My van is there. It's handicapped accessible and fully equipped. I'll need it to drive home."

The doctor looked back at Norman with an exasperated grimace. He shook his head and gave a quick shrug. Then, he turned without making a comment and walked out of the room.

Chapter 23

The phone rang twice.

"Hello," a deep voice said.

"Matt Winston?" asked Gallagher.

"Who's this?"

"You came to my office looking for me."

"Gallagher?"

"Right."

"Yes, I'm trying to reach Kate. I need to talk to her."

"Why?"

"That's between us. It has nothing to do with you."

"Then why did you come to my office?"

"I thought you might know where I could find her. No one seems to know anything about her. Seems like she's vanished all of a sudden."

"Doesn't Kate still hold a restraining order against you?"

Matt hesitated. Gallagher heard him heaving a big sigh.

"Look—I mean her no harm ..."

"That wasn't your approach a few years ago when you punched her around."

"You weren't there—you wouldn't know what really happened."

"I know enough to say that if we ever meet, you'll be sorry you ever hurt her."

Silence. A long pause. Another deep exhale. Finally, Matt spoke.

"Look, I just have a few questions for her."

"Sorry, I can't help you. I don't know where you can find Kate."

A true statement, but an evasive one, nonetheless, that Gallagher hoped would put an end to the conversation.

Matt jumped in quickly to prevent Gallagher from clicking off the call.

"Wait. Where are you? Can we meet somewhere to talk about this?"

His voice sounded desperate.

"Sorry, Matt. My advice to you is to respect Kate's wishes and observe that restraining order. If you don't stay away from her, you're either gonna deal with me or end up in jail."

Matt's voice grew louder as he yelled into the phone.

"Don't hang up! I need to ask you something important. What do you know about the baby?"

Stunned by the question, Gallagher held the phone away from his ear.

My god, he knows!

Gallagher looked down at the keypad. He said nothing in reply as he pushed the "end" button and finished the call.

Chapter 24

11:35 am

Despite the distraction of his call to Matt Winston, Gallagher made it to the sheriff's barracks in less time than expected. He walked in and gave his name to the officer at the desk. The officer looked down at a list of names and nodded.

"May I see your ID, Mr. Gallagher?"

Gallagher slid his driver's license through the opening in the plexiglass window. The officer studied the license for a few seconds and slid it back.

The door buzzed.

Gallagher walked in.

"I'm here to see Deputy Norris," he said.

"You've got him," said the deputy. "Just stand over here for a second."

Gallagher stood off to the side by an empty desk awaiting further instructions. Norris took a call at the window and ignored him, now oblivious to his presence. A few minutes passed. Two other deputies walked by. One of them leaned over toward Norris.

"We're going to Little Chuck's to pick up some lunch. Need anything?"

"No, I'm all set," he said, as he glanced down at the sports page of a folded newspaper. Gallagher finally caught his attention and gave him a look. Norris waved his hand and held up an index finger.

"Just wait there, sir. I'll be right with you."

No sense of urgency around here.

Gallagher fumed.

Finally, Deputy Norris pointed to a small office off to the right. "We can talk over there," he said.

Gallagher followed him into the office and took a seat in front of the desk. Norris sat down and stared across at him.

Norris hardly smiled. "You made it here pretty quickly after Gar's phone call," he said.

"When it's a matter of life or death, I usually hurry," said Gallagher. "I would hope you do the same."

"Which life and death matter are you referring to?"

"The murder of Cindy Kraemer and the disappearance of her daughter, Hayley and my ex-wife Kate McSurdy."

"I can assure you, Mr. Gallagher that we're doing everything we can. Do you have any evidence that will assist us in this case?"

"Who's in charge of this investigation?"

"That would be Sheriff Sanchez."

"I want to see him."

"Sorry, he's not available."

"I don't think you heard me," said Gallagher loudly. "I want to see him now!"

A man emerged from an office to the left. Tall, about six-foot-two, wearing a neatly pressed uniform. He looked to be in his mid-fifties and had an athletic build.

He stepped to the entrance of the small office and looked directly at Gallagher with a forced smile.

"Sheriff Sanchez. What's the problem?"

"I'm here about the Hayley Kraemer case. A woman is dead, my ex-wife and a little girl are missing, and your deputy here is wasting my time."

Sanchez dropped his smile and backed away. He stood rigidly for a second.

"Your name, sir?"

"Gallagher."

"Let's talk in my office," he said.

He turned and walked toward a larger room with an open door. Gallagher followed him in. Sanchez motioned to a chair in front of a desk.

Gallagher sat down.

Sanchez closed the door and circled around to his chair.

"So you're trying to find your ex-wife?" asked Sanchez.

"Yes—and maybe I'm trying to make sure that finding her is also at the top of your list."

Sanchez ignored the dig.

"Do you have any ideas about her disappearance, Mr. Gallagher?"

"You can drop the 'Mister.' But no, I don't. In fact, I've got the same question for you."

Gallagher shot an icy stare at Sanchez.

Sanchez caught the look, leaned back, and crossed his legs.

"Unfortunately, we have no leads and very few clues in this case. It seems like she and the little girl vanished into thin air."

"Captain Hartman from the Townsend police thinks that Kate may have kidnapped Hayley. What's your take on that?"

Sanchez laughed. "Yes, I heard you were snooping around the Kraemer house yesterday and Hartman brought you in for questioning."

"So you know all about it?" asked Gallagher, caught off guard by Sanchez' knowledge of yesterday's events at the Townsend Police Station.

"Of course. I received a full report. Jim Hartman's a rather intense cop, but he means well. The Townsend police are just monitoring activities at the Kraemer house. We're in charge of the investigation into the missing persons."

"We're eight days into this. What do you have so far?"

"Like I said—not much. But rest assured, this case is a top priority for us, and we have officers working on it night and day."

A typical press conference response—bland and non-committal. Gallagher wasn't buying it.

"Working night and day? You could have fooled me. Seems like a pretty casual atmosphere around here. What about Cindy Kraemer's murder? And her husband's death a few weeks ago? Can't you see that all of this is tied together?"

His voice grew louder as his frustration with Sanchez's indifference began to show. Gallagher fought to hold himself in check.

Sanchez didn't reply. Instead he took a sip from a bottle of water and rocked slightly in his chair as if measuring Gallagher's questions and waiting to see if he had anything more to say. Gallagher simply returned his stare.

A mini-stalemate developed.

Gallagher wasn't about to give in.

Finally, Sanchez unfolded his legs and sat up in his chair. He picked up a pen, tapped it on his desk a few times, and then held it loosely in his right hand. He pursed his lips and nodded. He appeared to have no intention to write anything down on the pad in front of him. Rather, he just needed a prop in his hand in order to get back into this discussion.

"Look—Gallagher," he started slowly. "You've got to give us some credit here that we know what we're doing. Finding Hayley Kraemer is the number-one objective of every officer on this force. We also want to find your ex-wife. Her role, if any, in Hayley's disappearance is still unclear. We don't know if she had any motives…"

"She had no motives," Gallagher interrupted. "It's obvious that Hayley and Kate were abducted."

"Well, we know that's a strong possibility, but at this point we have no proof that an abduction occurred."

"When you checked the Kraemer house for clues, what did you find?" asked Gallagher, remaining careful not to tip his hand but still showing a high degree of agitation.

"It appeared that they left on short notice," said Sanchez.

He coughed once and cleared his throat.

"Of course, the rooms could have been staged—carefully

orchestrated in a way to make it look like an abduction."

Another annoying jab, but Gallagher chose to let it pass. Instead he continued to press for answers.

"Any prints or signs of forced entry?" he asked.

"We dusted for prints on every doorway and in the study where it appeared that someone had gone through the desk. Nothing. The place was clean. Well—clean except for prints apparently belonging to the Kraemers and those that belonged to Kathryn McSurdy. We got a copy of your ex-wife's prints from that incident in Boston a while ago. You know the incident I mean—when she shot that guy three times in the back."

Sanchez' sarcasm was the last straw.

"Cut it out, Sanchez," said Gallagher.

"Hey—it's a matter of public record. I know she was completely exonerated. But in our line of work, we have to consider the whole picture. Most women would have just fired one bullet. A woman who fires three bullets shows a certain level of determination to get the job done. Maybe she's the type of woman who knows what she wants and doesn't let anything get in her way."

Gallagher rolled his eyes skyward.

"You mean, like kidnapping a three-year-old child?"

"We hear about cases like this all the time. Women who give a child up for adoption are often in turmoil and filled with regret. Years later, they make up their mind that they want the child back. They become irrational. Next thing you know, the police are involved."

Gallagher shook his head in utter disbelief.

"You've been talking too much to Captain Hartman. He's got the same ridiculous theory."

"We have to consider all the possibilities. You're a private investigator. You know this yourself."

The room became quiet again.

Another impasse.

This time Gallagher broke the ice.

"Let's go back to the beginning. How many unmarked police cars do you have in the sheriff's department?" he asked.

The question caught Sanchez off guard. He shifted in his chair and took another sip of water.

"Oh—probably six or eight. They're our oldest vehicles, and usually one or two of them are in the shop for repairs. What's the relevance?"

Sanchez's brow furrowed, and he rested his chin on his left hand. He tapped the pen lightly on the desk.

"Don Kraemer was attacked and bitten by a pit bull while he was jogging on the Wabash Heritage Trail. After the attack, he had a confrontation with the owner of the dog and demanded his ID. Then, Don saw an unmarked police car drive away from a pickup truck that the owner jumped into. Later on, Don found out that the dog's owner lied about his identity. He was trying to conceal his reason for being in that area at the time of the dog's attack. I believe that Don Kraemer contracted rabies from that dog, and I'll bet his autopsy report shows rabies as the cause of his death. And, furthermore, I'll bet that the officer in that unmarked police car can lead us to Kate and Hayley. Their abduction is part of some sort of cover-up. There's something big going on here—something that people are desperate to keep quiet. Cindy Kraemer figured it out and ended up dead."

Sanchez sat up and flipped his pen to the right side of the desk.

"You're making a pretty large leap here, Gallagher. And you're accusing a department with an impeccable record of public service and honesty. Do you have any proof about all of this?"

"Not yet. But for starters, why don't you request the autopsy report on Don Kraemer? Or, have you read it already?"

Sanchez shook his head.

"No, I haven't seen it. But I'll get it today."

Then, he curled his lower lip and shrugged his shoulders.

"Rabies, huh? No one ever mentioned that to us before. We were told he died of complications from a stroke."

"True. But I believe it was all brought on by a rabies infection. Norman Kraemer also told me that his brother had made several trips to the police to seek help in finding the owner of the dog. Did he ever come to the sheriff's office?"

"No—not that I know of. I never met Don Kraemer or even heard of him until this case broke open. Our records show nothing about him. But I'd be careful putting any stock into anything his brother Norman says. He's a bit of a whack-job."

Gallagher hardly let Sanchez finish his answer when he jumped in with another question.

"What about Cindy Kraemer's murder? Where do you stand with that investigation?"

The abrupt change of subjects again threw Sanchez for a

few seconds, but he rebounded with a firm answer.

"As Hartman told you, she died of blunt force trauma to the head. We don't know if she was killed outside of the car or while she was still behind the wheel. But after she was struck in the head, someone splashed gasoline around the interior of the car and set it on fire just as it began to roll off the side of the road."

"No witnesses?"

"None. It's a pretty quiet road at night."

"Any findings at the scene?"

"Nothing."

"What about the interior of the car? Anything you can go on?"

"The fire pretty much destroyed any evidence that would have been left in the cabin of the car. Our forensics team at the lab is still looking at it. But so far, they've come up with nothing new."

"So, where do you go from here?"

Sanchez smiled. "Maybe I should be asking you the same question?"

"I'm going to keep searching until I find Kate and Hayley."

"I figured you would. I can assure you that the sheriff's department will be doing the same. But you've got to understand—we have more resources than you do. Anything you find—any clue to their disappearance—you've got to give it to us. If they've been abducted, you won't be able to free them by yourself. You need us."

"Don't worry. I get it."

"And I'll do my best to keep you updated on our progress."

"Do more than just your best, Captain. I can be a big help to you."

"Gallagher, I know where you're coming from. You've got a personal stake here. You want immediate results and to be in on this case the whole way. But you know how it goes. Regulations just don't allow me to let you ride shotgun in a cruiser with one of my deputies. Let us handle it."

Gallagher stood up. He had nothing more to say.

Sanchez forced a weak smile. He rose from his chair and extended his hand.

"I'll check on that autopsy report and give you a call," he said.

Gallagher shook his hand.

"Thanks," he said.

He handed one of his cards to Sanchez.

"My cell number is on the back. Call me 24/7. Anything you find, I want to know."

Then he turned and walked out of the office.

Gallagher checked his watch—12:20 pm. The minutes kept ticking away, and he was no closer to finding Kate and Hayley.

Chapter 25

Gallagher sat in the front seat of his rental car and punched the address of Clarkson Animal Hospital into his GPS.

"Calculating route," said a woman's electronic voice.

Within seconds, he turned out of the parking lot of the sheriff's barracks and headed toward State Road 38 East. Desperate for an answer, Gallagher had decided to play a hunch. He hoped he could find it in a place where someone would take a very sick dog—a dog with rabies.

Gallagher drove along almost mindlessly, following the directions of the woman's voice on the GPS. He flipped on the radio. The sound of Bruce Springsteen's *Save My Love* blared through the speakers. The lyrics grabbed at him.

His thoughts drifted back to his last days together with Kate. The weeks before had been filled with stress and tension. Their relationship—once so vibrant and electric—had become strained and distant.

Unplugged.

He had struggled to get close to her, to discuss her feelings, to heal the hurt.

But she had pushed him away—both physically and emotionally.

Gallagher knew she had been scarred by the shooting incident. Kill someone? Kate had told him that, in her wildest dreams, she never imagined that she would take such action. But their lives had been threatened. On one harrowing night, she had been forced to kill a man—a horrible man—to save Gallagher's life.

But after the shooting, the threat persisted.

The mastermind behind the plot against Gallagher was still alive, free from arrest or indictment. The FBI had gotten caught up in political correctness. No charges had been filed; no warnings had been issued; no protection had been offered. Fearing for Kate's safety, Gallagher had smothered her with his own security blanket. He had stayed with her nearly every moment, overreacting to every sound in the driveway and to every visitor at the door. In his mind, deadly danger lurked all around them. He was determined to keep her safe.

But his actions had had a reverse effect. Instead of feeling closer to Gallagher, Kate had begged for space. She had the need to feel free. Perhaps she needed a way out?

She had begun to openly question her decision to marry a private investigator—someone whose choice of cases seemed to immerse both of them in danger and threaten their future. How could they raise a family? Would he ever give up this life and settle down to a normal existence?

They had drifted further apart.

Their nights had become filled with emptiness. She had

stayed alone in the bedroom; he had slept on the couch.

For Gallagher, the entire situation had become intolerable. He had become fed up with the FBI's inability to take action. He had decided to eliminate the threat on his own.

Permanently.

Secretly.

In a manner that could only be accomplished by a person of his considerable skill and talent.

In a way that could never be traced back to him.

Gallagher had never discussed his plan with Kate or anyone else. Some things are just never discussed. That way, there are no worries that someone else will be compromised or forced to talk to the authorities.

Another way to protect her?

Yes.

He had no other option.

He wouldn't allow anyone to threaten her again.

Then, the story of a car bombing incident in Las Vegas had broken on television and in the newspapers—the mysterious and unsolved assassination of an underworld boss.

Who had been responsible?

What had been the motive?

The police had been stumped.

No answers were ever found.

Kate had read the story. She had said nothing. She had asked no questions. But she knew. No explanation had been needed. Once again, they had been at the center of a violent and deadly event. Gallagher may have eliminated the threat to their lives, but their union had suffered irreparable harm.

Gallagher had tried to reach out to her—to attempt to rebuild their future. But their emotional struggles had continued. He had wondered how it would come to an end. He had feared that he would lose her forever.

Then one night, while he slept on the couch, he felt her hand on his face. She leaned over and kissed him.

Softly.

Tenderly.

No words had been spoken. She had rested her head on his chest and caressed his neck. Then she had led him back to the bedroom.

He remembered lying next to her naked body, feeling her smooth and warm skin once again.

But that was Kate—always warm.

At times it seemed like a fire burned within her.

After weeks of ice, their bodies had melted together passionately that night. Kate's body had come alive with a new level of arousal and urgency.

She had pulled him closer, desperate to feel him within her in order to satisfy a deep longing.

Perhaps to create a lasting memory.

An hour later, as they rested quietly on the bed, he had looked at her.

"*A chuisle mo chroi*," he had said, reciting again the Irish phrase "pulse of my heart." Words that always perfectly summed up his feelings for her.

He loved her more than ever.

"*Mo chuisle,*" she had said softly. But her voice had quivered. Her eyes had filled with tears. She had looked away.

Nothing more had been said, but he had known what was about to happen.

He was powerless to stop her.

The next day she was gone.

And his life had been torn apart.

———

Then the music stopped.

"You have arrived at your destination," said the woman's voice.

Gallagher snapped back to reality.

He ran his hand through his hair and shook his head.

He looked up at the sign: Clarkson Animal Hospital.

He turned into the parking lot.

A black, unmarked police car had followed him all the way and pulled off the main road and parked on a side street with a direct view of the hospital.

Chapter 26

Four hours earlier

Three short knocks on the door.

The usual early morning signal.

Kate scooped Hayley up into her arms and walked to the rear of the small house.

"Come with me, sweetheart. It's time to play our little game of hide and seek."

This had become the daily routine. Kate's standing orders were simple and straightforward. When she heard the knocks at the door each morning, she had to move away toward the far wall of the small sitting room with her back to the front door.

She was not allowed to look out the door.

Never to get a glimpse of the surroundings or a hint where they were being held captive.

On the night they were abducted, she had arrived wearing a blindfold. Hayley had clutched her arms around Kate's neck and shivered with fear. But they had not been harmed. Once they were brought inside the house, Kate's blindfold had been removed. The leader of the group—a short, stocky man—had bluntly explained the rules. They were being held in a secret location. No harm would come to them if Kate cooperated. No resistance or questions allowed. Daily provisions of food, milk, and other necessities would be provided. He promised their eventual release. If Kate tried to escape, he could no longer guarantee her safety or that of Hayley.

End of discussion.

Kate had no choice. She could not let anyone harm Hayley. For the eight days of their captivity, she had cooperated completely.

She heard the rattling sound of the bolt lock and latch. The door screeched open, and a man burst in with a boisterous roar.

"Good morning! Diego is here! I bring you lots of good-ies today. Where is that special little girl? The one who likes chocolate candies?"

Kate held Hayley in her arms and continued facing the rear wall until she heard the door close. Then, she turned around and put Hayley down at her side. Hayley clung to her leg and eyed their animated visitor suspiciously.

Diego placed two grocery bags on the kitchen table and began to unload its contents into the refrigerator.

"See—I have milk for you and some Cheerios. Diego knows you like Cheerios."

Then, he lifted a large, ripe peach from the bag.

"See—I have fresh fruit for you, too. Diego picked this peach 'specially for you."

He crouched down and extended his hand toward the little girl who buried her face to the side of Kate's leg. Then she peeked around the corner with her thumb in her mouth to see what other goodies might come out of the bags. Kate reached down and took her hand.

"Come with me, Hayley. Let's make a nice breakfast for you. Cheerios topped with some slices of that delicious-looking peach."

As Kate began to prepare Hayley's breakfast, Diego continued his excited verbal barrage—like a Santa Claus taking toys out of his Christmas sack.

"Oh, my! See what else I have for you today. Some orange juice, animal crackers, and—" he paused for a few seconds to create greater dramatic emphasis. His eyes widened and he let out a mock gasp. "Aaah! Wait until you see these chocolate-chip cookies!"

Kate ignored the theatrical display and began to slice the peach over a bowl filled with Cheerios. Hayley continued to cling to Kate's pant leg, keeping her distance from the short, stocky man. The shyness associated with her selective mutism prevented her from uttering a response.

When the breakfast was ready, Kate took Hayley over to the small table. Obviously hungry, Hayley climbed onto her seat and began eating.

Kate walked back toward the kitchen counter where Diego continued to empty the contents of the bags into the refrigerator and the small cabinet above the counter. His pants pocket bulged on the right side with a heavy object. Kate assumed he carried a weapon—most likely a gun.

She approached him cautiously.

As she grew near, Diego flashed a wide, gap-toothed smile at Kate.

"And what do I have for the sweet Señora?" he asked, directing the question to himself as he reached into the last bag.

Kate darted a harsh look toward him.

"Diego—or whatever your name is—I doubt that it's really Diego. You can drop the fake Latino accent and this little charade you put on every morning," she said. "Just tell me how much longer we're going to be held here."

The man looked up in surprise—like a schoolboy who got caught with his hand in the cookie jar. His smile gave way to a partially opened mouth. He inhaled and shook his head as if ready to protest Kate's accusation. But he seemed to change his mind. He exhaled deeply and tilted his head to the side. Their eyes locked in a brief stare down.

"Look, lady. I wish you never got involved in this. But you were in the wrong place at the wrong time. Now you're gonna have to deal with it."

Kate didn't flinch. She stepped closer to him.

"What were you looking for in Cindy's house? Why couldn't you just go away after you found it and leave us alone?"

"You were a witness, lady. We couldn't afford to have a witness."

"I can still be a witness and identify you. I know your face."

Diego shrugged his shoulders and shook his head side to side. Then he flashed a sinister smile.

"You know my face? Maybe you'd like to know more than just my face. Whaddya' say, Lady? Maybe me and you should get together … real close together."

Kate backed away slightly, not wanting this creep to put a hand on her. Diego stared at her for a few seconds and finally dropped the sinister smile. He looked away, as if pondering another thought.

"It won't matter if you know my face," he said. "I'm never coming back to this place again."

Kate ignored his thought and resumed her pressure for information. "Where's Cindy? What have you done to her?"

"Hey, lady—remember our deal here? No questions. Too many questions will get you and the little girl in trouble."

Kate lifted her hand and pointed her finger at the short, stocky man. At five foot six inches tall, she met him at eye level when she moved closer.

"If you ever do anything to hurt her, you'll be sorry."

He stepped back a little and returned her threat with an icy stare. He had lifted a jar of peanut butter from the bag and now lightly bounced it in his hand a few times. Was he about to use this jar as a weapon?

Kate's muscles became rigid. She felt a rush of adrenaline—ready to defend herself if necessary.

Then, he raised an eyebrow and, with a look of resignation, placed the jar on a shelf in the cabinet.

"You're talkin' tough, lady," he said. "Real tough."

His lips curled up in a wry smile.

"You have no idea how tough I can be. You better not even think about it," she said.

She'd made her steely resolve clear. She wasn't backing down.

He shrugged his shoulders again and emptied another small bag onto the counter—a tube of toothpaste, two toothbrushes, and a bar of soap. Then, he walked around the counter and stood face to face with Kate.

"Look, lady—if we wanted to hurt you, we would have done it the night we walked into that house. We didn't expect to find anyone there, least of all a little girl. We might be bad guys, but we don't hurt little girls."

Then with a smirk, he added, "At least not until they grow up."

Kate moved toward him angrily, "You bastard!"

Diego quickly flashed a knife.

"Stop right there, lady, or you're gonna be real sorry."

Kate backed away slowly, still fuming at him.

"What did you do to Cindy?"

Kate let the question hang there as she stared into his eyes.

The short, stocky man paused. He looked down at the floor, then across at Hayley who sat quietly eating her breakfast cereal.

"We didn't hurt Cindy. Someone else had to deal with her. Very unfortunate, but she kept pushing and wouldn't let up."

He paused again, apparently seeking the right words.

"You see, lady—this is all about time. We needed time to get everything in place. She was going to interfere with an important schedule. We couldn't afford to let her make any trouble for us."

He stepped closer, now nearly nose-to-nose with Kate.

"And if you want to stay alive, you better not do anything to fuck up our schedule. We're almost done here. Just a few more days, and you'll be free. You and the little girl could walk out of here without a scratch. Or maybe you come with us? There's a lot of guys who'd pay big bucks to spend some quality time with you. Maybe even me. But I won't have to pay a dime. You'd be all mine, free of charge. It's all up to you, lady. Got it?"

Kate ignored the sinister threat. She didn't back away.

"You must know that by now, people are searching for us. They'll find us. You'll go to prison or be killed by the police. Let us go now and get away while you can."

He smirked and gave a quick laugh.

"You're not going anywhere until the time is right. They will find you, and if you play your cards right, you'll be alive. But we'll be long gone."

He lifted his left hand to the front of his mouth and blew across his palm.

"Like smoke vanishing in the air, we'll be long gone—never to be seen again."

Kate said nothing. She stepped away. She walked over to the small table, crouched down next to Hayley and kissed her on the top of her head.

"How's your breakfast, sweetheart? Did you like the peaches?"

Hayley lifted a spoonful toward her mouth and nodded. Her little legs swung merrily back and forth below the chair.

The door to the cabin suddenly creaked. Kate looked up. She heard the sounds of the latch closing and the lock being fastened.

The man who called himself Diego had disappeared.

Chapter 27

The vibrating cell phone jiggled his pants pocket. Matt Winston reached in, pulled out the phone, and looked at the screen—"Joel Braxton." He plopped down on the bed in his one-bedroom apartment and leaned back on a pillow while resting one leg on the floor. He held the phone to his ear.

"Yes, Joel. What is it?"

"I've got some news for you. In fact, I've got quite a bit of news."

"I hope it's good."

"Do you have a pen and a piece of paper? You might want to write some of this down."

"Just a second."

Matt grabbed a ballpoint pen from the nightstand. He stood up and walked over to his dresser. He opened the top drawer and lifted out a small writing pad.

"Okay, I'm ready," Matt said, as he leaned against the dresser and cradled the phone next to his left ear.

"I've gathered some information from a number of sources. But they're very reliable. You can bank on them."

"Okay, I'm listening."

"Kathryn Daisy McSurdy had a baby girl at Lafayette General Hospital in Lafayette, Indiana three and a half years ago. The baby's name is Hayley."

"Hayley?" asked Matt gently.

His mind drifted away from the conversation. "Hayley—" he repeated. He could now put a name to the child who had consumed his thoughts for the past few days.

Braxton left him little time for daydreams.

"Yes, Hayley. But she was adopted by a couple named Donald and Cynthia Kraemer of Townsend, Indiana, shortly after the birth. The baby was discharged from the hospital under the name Hayley Kraemer. But then the story gets very interesting."

"Yes?"

"Donald Kraemer passed away a few weeks ago. Young man; only forty-five years of age. No cause of death listed in the newspaper. The article just said 'after a brief illness.'"

"Oh?"

"But then his wife Cynthia, who went by Cindy, was found dead in her car on a highway in Indiana. No cause of death listed, but the police are still investigating it as a homicide."

Matt slumped down on his bed, cradling the phone against his ear with his left hand while jotting the facts onto the writing pad as it rested on his lap.

"Jesus! What about Hayley? Did anything happen to her?"

"No, she wasn't in the car. But she vanished before Cindy's body was discovered. The police issued an Amber Alert for Hayley and an all-points bulletin for Kathryn McSurdy. So far, neither one of them has been found. There's speculation that they could have been abducted or possibly killed. Or maybe Kate went into hiding with Hayley? It's a real mystery."

Silence.

Stunned by the last words, Matt said nothing.

"You there, Matt?" asked Braxton.

After a few seconds, Matt responded. His voice choked with emotion.

"I can't believe this. What could have happened to them? And the couple that adopted her? Both dead? It doesn't make any sense."

"Well, there's another wrinkle to all of this. Your friend, Gallagher, hasn't been seen around here for a few days, and no one's talking about his whereabouts. I tried to get it out of his secretary, but she clammed up. My guess is that he's out in Indiana. He's either involved, or he's trying to find out who's involved in the disappearance of his ex-wife."

"Gallagher?"

"That's right."

"You think he'd go after Kate?"

"Probably not. But the word on the street is that he was pretty depressed when she left him. You never know. Some guys crack under that kind of pressure."

Matt said nothing. He sat quietly trying to digest all the facts that Braxton had just delivered. An inner rage began to churn, and he struggled to control the thoughts of revenge that suddenly reached a boiling point.

Braxton sounded impatient with his lack of response.

"Matt?" he asked.

"Yeah, I'm here," Matt barked.

"What are you going to do now?"

"I'm not sure. I've got a lot to think about."

"Well, one thing I should make you aware of. The disappearance of Kate and your little daughter is an investigation that's being handled by the sheriff's office in Indiana and, by this time, probably even the State Police and the FBI. It's strictly a police matter. There's no way I can get involved any further. So I really can't do anything else to help you."

"I understand."

"But if you have any questions, I may be able to gather up some information from some of my contacts."

Matt's thoughts continued to stray from the conversation.

After a brief delay, he responded, "Okay, thanks."

"I'll drop a final bill for my services in the mail. I'm sure you'll find it to be a fair payment for what I had to do on your behalf."

Matt grunted. Then he blurted out a nasty retort.

"Just send the bill; I'll take care of it."

Braxton failed to pick up on the venom in the reply.

"Okay, Matt. I wish you luck with this. I sincerely hope it has a good outcome. And I caution you about taking any action on your own. This is serious business—dangerous stuff. Let the police handle it."

"Thanks."

Matt clicked off the phone and angrily threw it down on his bed. He flung himself beside the phone and leaned his head back on the pillow. He placed his hands over his eyes and took several deep breaths. His mind churned with dozens of crazy scenarios. He just couldn't sit back and wait for further events to unfold.

Where should he begin?

How could he find the child that had been taken away from him?

Was she still alive?

It was all Kate's fault. She had no right to do this.

To give her away without a word—without his consent.

She had placed his little girl in danger.

Now, she was missing.

No, he couldn't wait; he had to act.

I'll get even with her for doing this!

Matt got up from his bed and walked over to his dresser. He opened the second drawer. He reached into the back of the drawer and pushed some workout clothes aside to reveal a rectangular, black box with a smooth vinyl cover. He removed the box and placed it on top of the dresser. He lifted the cover of the box and took out the only item—a 9mm Glock automatic pistol.

Matt held the gun in his hand for more than a minute. He hadn't even looked at it in years. Now he studied it carefully. Wild possibilities continued to race through his mind. Slowly and deliberately, he put the gun back into the case.

Matt sat down with his laptop computer and Googled "Airlines servicing Lafayette, Indiana." He stared at the monitor for a few seconds.

Then, he walked over to his closet and took out a travel suitcase on wheels. He was energized as he hurriedly grabbed shirts and slacks off their hangers and began to pack. He picked up his phone, punched in a number, and then cradled the phone against his shoulder as he continued to shove clothes into his suitcase.

"In Boston, I need the number of US Airways reservations."

Chapter 28

Gallagher walked through the main entrance of the Clarkson Animal Hospital and stopped at the front desk, but there was no one on duty.

He looked at his watch.

Too late for lunch. Where is everybody?

He felt like he was lagging behind. His impatience and frustration had begun to get the best of him.

He looked around. A woman sat on a bench in the corner of the reception area holding a white bichon frise. The little dog perked up and barked. Gallagher walked over and petted the top of the dog's head. The dog wriggled its head excitedly and licked his hand.

"Is there anyone working at the desk today?" he asked the woman.

"Oh, she just stepped away. She should be back in a minute."

"Great little dog," he said.

"Thanks," said the woman. "Just brought her in for her annual check-up."

"I've got a Golden."

"Oh, they're wonderful."

"Yes. I miss her. Had to put her in a kennel for a few days while I'm out here to—," he paused. "—out here on business."

The woman smiled and nodded.

"Oh, look. She just returned," she said, pointing to the main desk.

"Thanks."

Gallagher walked over. A young woman wearing a navy-blue lab coat looked up. Her name tag read "Lori."

"Yes, can I help you?" she asked.

Gallagher leaned over the counter. "I'd like to speak to the chief veterinarian."

"Are you a salesman?"

"No, I'm actually a private investigator. I have some questions about a case I'm working on."

Gallagher reached across and handed one of his cards to Lori. She studied it for a few seconds and looked up.

"All the way from Boston?" she asked.

"Yes."

"I love Boston."

"Been there?"

"No. But I love all the TV shows and movies they make there. Someday I'd like to take a trip back East. When I do, for sure I'll go to Boston."

She stood up, still staring at the card, and quickly switched gears.

"Dr. Thibeault is on today. I'll see if he can talk to you."

"Is he the chief veterinarian?"

"No. Dr. Hinderstein is the chief. He's off today. But Dr. Thibeault is one of the managing partners. I think he's in between surgeries, so he may be free now."

She walked to the back of the front-desk area and through a door leading to the treatment rooms. A few minutes went by. Gallagher stood by the desk and waited. The constant delays kept gnawing at him. The bichon frise sat up and barked twice. Gallagher turned around and smiled. The little dog had broken up the tension of waiting.

"I think she wants to be petted a bit more," he said.

The woman holding the bichon laughed.

"Yes, I think she's made a new friend."

A pair of automatic doors to the left of the front desk swung open and interrupted the friendly banter. A man walked out. He had a tan, weathered face and wore a light-blue scrub suit. A nose-cone mask dangled by a loose elastic band around his neck. Wisps of gray hair extended out from the sides of his surgeon's cap. Gallagher estimated that he was in his mid-sixties.

"Lori said you had some questions?" he asked.

"Yes. Is there somewhere we can talk?"

"Well, I'm about to go into a surgery. What's it all about?"

His eyes narrowed, and he gave Gallagher a quizzical look.

"My name's Gallagher. I'm investigating a missing persons case—a woman and a three-year-old little girl. I believe a critical clue to their disappearance involves a dog with rabies. That dog may have been treated here."

"You mean euthanized here. We wouldn't 'treat' an animal

with rabies."

"Right. Euthanized."

The skeptical look subsided. He extended his hand.

"I'm Dr. Chuck Thibeault. Come back to my office. I've only got a few minutes, but we can talk there."

Dr. Thibeault pushed a large, round button on the wall. The automatic doors swung open. He walked through, and Gallagher followed.

Dr. Thibeault led him to a small office to the left of a sign that read "Operating Suite." He motioned toward a chair.

"Nothing fancy here, but have a seat. I don't know how much I can legally tell you, but let's see what you want to know."

Gallagher sat down. He noticed a picture on the desk—an attractive blonde woman standing behind Dr. Thibeault with her arms around his neck. The caption on the picture frame read "To my Babycakes." Gallagher was tempted, but decided not to ask.

Instead, he wasted no time getting right to the point.

"Have you had a pit bull named Caesar come into this hospital with rabies in the past two weeks?"

Dr. Thibeault hesitated. The quizzical look returned.

"Cases of rabies are quite rare around here."

He paused, as if waiting for Gallagher to lay a few more cards on the table.

"If they're so rare, you'd certainly remember a recent case. In fact, I'd guess it would be the main topic of conversation among the veterinarians on the staff. Not so?"

"Yes. We're obligated to report such cases to the county

sheriff's department so they can investigate any possible human contact with the rabid animal. We ..."

Gallagher held his hand forward in a halt signal.

"Forgive me for interrupting, doctor. But let's get back to my main question. Did a pit bull named Caesar come into this hospital with rabies?"

Dr. Thibeault shifted his weight in his chair. He reached up and slipped the surgeon's cap off his head. He raised an eyebrow and looked across at Gallagher. He studied him for a few seconds and then spoke in a harsh monotone.

"We've been advised by the police not to discuss this case with anyone."

"By which police?"

"The county sheriff's office."

"Did they say why?"

"We were told it was a top-secret case and that we had to maintain strict confidentiality about all of the details."

Gallagher leaned forward.

"Chuck—can I call you Chuck?"

"Of course."

"I see from the photograph that you have a wife. Any kids?"

"Yes, my wife and I have been married for almost forty years. We have two daughters. In fact, I'm also a grandfather."

"Then you'll understand what I'm about to say. My ex-wife is missing. Circumstances may have caused us to be apart, but we still love each other. She's not only missing, but her life and the life of her child may be in extreme danger. They've been abducted by people who have already killed one person and may not hesitate to kill more. The owner of that pit bull may lead me to the place where they're being held. The police haven't found them, but I can. This is no time to dwell on protocol."

"But ..."

"Chuck, if one of your daughters went missing, what would you do? Would you explore every avenue to find her or sit around and wait for the police?"

Dr. Thibeault took a deep breath. He looked at his wrist, and then realized he wasn't wearing his watch. Then he looked up at the clock on the wall.

"I have to get back to the OR."

Gallagher kept pressing him.

"Chuck, I need to know whatever you've got. You don't want blood on your hands if something happens to them."

Dr. Thibeault squeezed his lips together. A hard squeeze. He took a deep breath. Then he heaved a big sigh as he rubbed his hands on the sides of his cheeks. He looked like a man in turmoil.

"Look, whatever I tell you is between us—off the record."

"Completely."

Dr. Thibeault leaned forward, folded his hands and put them on the desk.

"About three weeks ago, early in the evening, I was just about to leave. One of my junior associates was working the night clinic and came in to catch me before I left. A guy had come in here with a pit bull, foaming at the mouth. The dog was in rough shape. Nearly listless. I knew right away the animal was rabid."

"Tell me about the owner."

"Seemed to be Latino. Short, stocky guy. He wore a thick gold necklace and looked like maybe a laborer. I explained that we had to euthanize the dog. He seemed sad about it, but I don't think he expected anything else."

"Did you get his name?"

"No. We had to act fast—get fully gowned, face shields, protective eyewear—the whole nine yards. I told him it wasn't safe for him to be in the treatment room with us and asked him to wait in the reception area. I explained that we had to do a pretty extensive interview with him when we were done to make sure the dog hadn't bitten anyone. Any person with intimate contact—petting the dog's face, coming in contact with his saliva, etc.—could be at risk for contracting rabies. He agreed to wait. I heard him say, 'Poor Caesar.' We took the dog into the OR; that was the last I saw of the guy."

"You mean he just took off?"

"More or less, yes."

"What do you mean?"

"Well, he went out to the front desk. Our secretary gave him some forms to fill out and told him the fee for the euthanization would be three hundred dollars. She also told him he'd have to agree to have the dog's remains autopsied for a definitive diagnosis. Then, while she gathered a few forms and a clipboard, he bolted out the door."

"What did she do?"

"She didn't dare try to stop him. In fact, she said she was a little afraid of the guy. But she did a pretty smart thing. She got his license plate and a description of his truck—a dark blue pickup—before he drove out of the parking lot. One of those smaller pickups—a Tacoma."

"You gave it to the police?"

"Yes. A deputy from the sheriff's office came by. We gave all the information to him—the license, a description of the owner, everything we could remember."

"Then what happened?"

"The next day, I got a call from the sheriff's office. It was one of the senior officers. He's the one who told me that this was a top secret, classified investigation being conducted by the sheriff's office. We were not allowed to release any of the information to the press or the public."

"You wouldn't still happen to have that license number, would you?"

Dr. Thibeault became quiet. He closed his eyes for a few seconds and then looked up at the ceiling.

"I don't know, Gallagher. You're not going to bring down my whole career with this, are you?"

Gallagher pleaded.

"Chuck, I know this is hard. But the lives of two people are hanging in the balance. What you do in the next few minutes could make a huge difference in saving them. I need that license number."

Dr. Thibeault pushed his chair back and exhaled deeply. He avoided Gallagher's eyes and shook his head in a near surrender.

"Shit. Why did I agree to talk to you? You're playing games with my conscience."

He sat quietly, shaking his head side to side. Gallagher waited, giving him time to sort out his troubled thoughts.

Finally, Dr. Thibeault sat up in his chair.

"No matter how I look at this, I know you're right," he said. "I've got to help. I just hope this doesn't come back to haunt me."

He reached into his drawer and took out a small note card. He pulled a brown case with his reading glasses from the side pocket of his scrub top and put the glasses on. He studied the information written on the note card for a few seconds. Then he took a pen and scribbled a few numbers and letters on a blank card.

"Here you go," he said. "Indiana plates—that's the number. And you don't remember where you got it."

He looked at Gallagher over the top of his reading glasses as he stretched his arm across the desk.

Gallagher reached over and took the card.

"Thanks, Chuck. I really appreciate your help."

Dr. Thibeault stood and threw his hands up in the air in a mock gesture of surrender.

"Okay—now that I've put myself in legal jeopardy, I'd better get back to work."

Gallagher shook his hand.

"Don't worry. I'd never reveal a source."

"If you do, I'm screwed."

Dr. Thibeault reacted to his own comment with a nervous laugh.

"One more question," asked Gallagher.

"Make it quick, I'm late getting back in there."

"The sheriff's officer who called you—what was his name?"

Dr. Thibeault winced.

"Oh, jeez—"

He rolled his eyes upward and appeared stumped. Then his memory kicked into gear.

"Wait a second—I never met him; just talked to him once on the phone. I think I wrote the name down."

He pulled open the same drawer where he had stored the note card with the license number. He rooted around through some loose papers and then pulled out a small piece of lined paper.

"Here it is," he said. "Sanchez—Captain Bob Sanchez. He's the officer who called."

Chapter 29

Gallagher hurried his steps as he walked to his car. He needed privacy for the phone call he was about to place. Time and time again, Phyllis Sax, his friend at the Massachusetts Registry of Motor Vehicles, had proven to be an invaluable source of information. This time, he needed her help more than ever.

He reached the car in a near sprint, opened the door, and sat down behind the steering wheel. He took out his phone and pressed "7" on his speed-dial list. After two rings, her familiar voice answered.

"Commercial licenses, this is Phyllis," she said.

"Phyllis, how are you?"

A brief pause—then a boisterous response.

"Gallagher? Is this my once-every-six-months phone call?"

Her laugh turned into a loud roar.

He gave a flat response.

"Hey, I'm impressed that you always remember the sound of my voice."

"How could I forget you? My favorite private eye! How's Kate?"

Gallagher suddenly remembered that he had not spoken to Phyllis since his separation and divorce. This was not the right time to get into specifics about the problems in his personal life. Better to save it for another discussion. His tone turned serious.

"Phyllis, I can't go into details right now, but the lives of two people are in danger. I need your help in tracing a license plate to its owner."

She immediately recognized the gravity of his voice and dropped her playful banter.

"Massachusetts?" she asked.

"No. Indiana."

"Indiana? What the hell are you doing in Indiana?"

"It's a long story."

"Always is. But, okay—you sound a bit stressed. What's the tag number?"

"Indiana plates. Two, Two, Zero, White, X-ray, Mary."

"220WXM, right?"

"That's it. On a dark blue Toyota Tacoma."

"Okay, I'll see what I can do. It might take a while."

"Phyllis, this is urgent. I don't have a lot of time."

"Don't you have any police friends out there that could help you with this?"

"Phyllis, every cop I meet in Indiana seems to have a problem with me. There's no one in the police department I can trust."

"Alright—don't worry. I'm on it. Keep your cell close; I'll be calling."

The phone clicked. She was gone. Gallagher took a deep breath and started the engine. His thoughts turned to Captain Bob Sanchez.

That lying bastard! He's involved in this up to his ears. But why?

Gallagher turned out of the parking lot and headed toward West Lafayette.

The unmarked police car remained parked on the side street for about thirty seconds while a few cars passed by. Then, it pulled out and followed Gallagher, staying out of view several car lengths behind.

Chapter 30

Gallagher's phone chimed within a few minutes of leaving the animal hospital.

Could Phyllis have gotten the information he needed so fast?

Not this time.

The name "Norman Kraemer" appeared on the screen.

Not such a bad alternative.

"Norman?" said Gallagher.

"Yeah. I'm home from the hospital already."

"Great work this morning. You should be in the movies."

Norman ignored the compliment. "Did you find anything in the house?" he asked.

"Actually, I did. Do the initials SRF mean anything to you?"

A long pause. Norman breathed heavily into the phone.

"SRF? No—'fraid I don't know anyone with those initials."

"How about a location or a business? Anything like that?"

Now a long groan.

"Sorry, man—I'm drawin' a blank. What makes you ask?"

"I'll fill you in later, Norman. What can you tell me about the sheriff's department in this county? Ever have anything to do with them?"

"Me? With the sheriff's office? Not personally. But I heard a lot of stuff about them. A guy I served with in the Gulf War worked there for a while after his discharge, 'til they finally got rid of him."

"Got rid of him? Why?"

"They said he wasn't a team player. He thought they were playin' fast and loose with the inventory. Some shady dealings goin' on. He asked a few too many questions, and next thing ya know he was lookin' for a new job."

"Do you keep in touch with this guy?"

"Off and on. Haven't talked to him in—oh—probably a year."

"But you know how to reach him?"

"Sure. Marty Homan. I've got his number if you want to talk to him sometime."

"Yes. I might want to do that. Are you going to be home later?"

Norman exhaled loudly.

"Where am I gonna go? Out on a date?"

Gallagher smiled.

"Good, Norman. I've got to check on a few things and then I'll stop by. Anything I can bring for you?"

"How 'bout some Bud Light?"

Gallagher chuckled to himself.

"Okay, my friend. Some Bud Light it'll be. See you later."

Chapter 31

The crush of phone calls to the *Lafayette Eagle-Tribune* office of Gar Kearney had finally subsided. Now, late in the afternoon, he prepared to leave his office for the day and head home for dinner. The phone rang again. He hesitated to pick it up, feeling that he had had his fill of crank calls and wild speculation for the day. His story on the disappearance of Hayley Kraemer had captured the imagination of the whacked-out conspiracy theorists among his readership. Nothing they offered was close to printable.

He grabbed his sport coat and turned toward the door. The phone kept ringing. Reluctantly, he gave in and picked it up on the fifth ring.

"Gar Kearney," he said. "I'm on my way out the door. This better be good."

"Gar—it's Gallagher."

"Gallagher!" he said, perking up. "How'd your meeting go?"

"Well, Deputy Norris tried to blow me off, but I did get a chance to speak to the guy in charge, Captain Sanchez. How well do you know him?"

Taken aback, Gar stammered, "Wha—Whaddya mean?"

"Like I said, how well do you know Sanchez?"

"Well, I wouldn't say we're best of friends—not exactly drinking buddies. But I have known him for quite a few years."

"Ever conduct an interview with him?"

"Not really. But I've been the lead reporter on a number of cases that he's handled. He's always been open and frank with me. What are you getting at? What's the problem?"

"He's covering something up."

"What?"

"He lied to me about Don Kraemer's death. He knows all about it. He personally spoke to someone at the animal hospital and tried to keep a lid on the rabies incident."

"Bob Sanchez? You can't be serious."

"Oh, yes. This is very serious business. And Sanchez is part of it. Don Kraemer stumbled onto something that day and triggered a deadly sequence of events. Now Kate and Hayley are caught up in it."

"My god! This is not good," said Gar as he tossed his jacket on the desk and plopped himself down in his chair. "A captain in the sheriff's office? This is really not good."

"Look, Gar—hang in there—I'm going to need your help."

"What can I do?"

"Call Sanchez. Make him think you're following up on your story. See what he has to say about my visit. Then ask him what he knows about Don Kraemer's death. Maybe he'll let something slip or get crossed up trying to cover his tracks."

A few empty seconds passed.

"Alright, I'll try. I'm not very good at playing actor. Might be hard to reach him now anyway. It's late in the day."

"Do whatever you can—leave a message—tell him it's important. Maybe he'll get back to you."

"Okay. I'll see what I can do."

"Gar—" Gallagher paused.

"Yes?"

"Keep pushing on this. We could be running out of time."

"Don't worry. I will."

"Thanks."

Another pause.

"If I come up with anything, can we meet somewhere?" asked Gar.

"Sure."

"Where?"

"Just call my cell. We'll find a place. Right now I'm just waiting for some information on a pickup truck that may lead me to the guy who owned that rabid dog. If I find him, I have a feeling I'll find Kate and Hayley."

"Okay. I'll be in touch as soon as I'm able to speak to Bob Sanchez."

"Remember—play it cool. Don't let him think you suspect anything. Just an investigative reporter following up on his story, okay?"

"No problem."

"By the way, any further thoughts on those initials, SRF?"

"Still nothing. But I'll keep checking. I'll let you know if I figure out what they mean."

Chapter 32

5:30 pm

It was already dark—the switch to standard time had been a week earlier—when Gallagher pulled up to his motel. Not a fancy place, but it was close to the Interstate and offered a clean room and a free breakfast: over-baked muffins and tasteless coffee. Just the thought of drinking the stuff again in the morning made him long for a cup of Brooklyn Coffee House Blend. Too bad his favorite coffee had not made it as far west as Indiana.

Gallagher had checked in on the previous night, following his run-in with the Townsend police. His room was on the ground floor near the far end of the motel.

Gallagher parked in a space in front of his door.

Exhausted and needing sleep, Gallagher's legs felt leaden. He trudged up to the door, inserted his key, and walked in to the totally dark room.

As he reached for the light switch to the right of the door, he noticed the open window on the far side of the room. He could feel the cool fall air as it blew through the wide-open window—a window he had closed when he left the motel this morning.

His heartbeat quickened.

He made a fast step to his right and reached for his Glock.

Too late.

The door slammed shut, and a man lunged toward him.

Gallagher arched away but felt a piercing, stinging pain in his side. A knife had slashed across his skin. Knocked off balance, Gallagher fell to the floor. He scrambled to retrieve his Glock.

No use.

The man pounced down on him.

Despite the rush of adrenaline to defend himself, Gallagher's mind seemed to slow down the action. He could barely see through the darkness but caught a glimpse of the man's arm rising with the knife, ready to plunge it into Gallagher's chest.

Gallagher arched upward and grabbed the man's arm with both hands and pulled his assailant down.

The two men grappled on the floor, each trying to gain an advantage. Gallagher finally rolled the man over on his side, keeping the hand with the knife extended and unable to strike. But the intruder retaliated with a crushing, backward elbow blow that struck Gallagher in the face.

Stunned, he fell back against the wall, and blood splattered from his nose.

His eyes watered, clouding his vision.

The man rose to his knees and lunged toward Gallagher with the knife.

Before the blade reached him, Gallagher flexed his knee and kicked upward, striking the charging man squarely in the jaw with the heel of his shoe. The man toppled to the floor with a loud groan. The knife flew out of his hand and landed harmlessly near the bed, far from the man's reach.

Gallagher gasped for air and pulled himself up to his knees, trying to gather the strength to subdue his stunned attacker. Blood oozed from the wound in Gallagher's abdomen. His shirt was soaked with blood and perspiration. More blood trickled down from his nose and mouth. He began to make a move toward the man who rolled over on his side and reached into his pocket.

Gallagher saw a gun come out, and he lunged forward and slammed the man down to the floor. The gun in the man's right hand slipped from his fingers and skidded out of his reach. Realizing that the gun was now closer to Gallagher, the man kicked and flailed wildly, trying to prevent Gallagher from reaching the weapon.

The desperate struggle continued. Gallagher's strength began to wane as he fought to breathe and his blood loss worsened. Still, he was within reach of the gun and could turn it on his assailant if he could get his hands on it. Recognizing his precarious position, the man frantically kicked out at the gun and pushed it further away from Gallagher.

Then, with a sudden burst of energy, the man broke out of Gallagher's hold, rose to his feet, and ran toward the window.

Gallagher slithered along the floor and grabbed the gun. He turned, looked up, and extended the pistol.

But before Gallagher could pull the trigger, the man dove out the window and disappeared into the night.

Chapter 33

The triage nurse in the emergency room lifted the towel away from the wound in Gallagher's side.

"You're lucky. It's not too deep, but it's going to need some stitches," she said with authority.

Clearly, this was not the first time she had seen a gash in the abdomen.

"I figured it needed stitches. That's why I came here," said Gallagher, lifting his head from the pillow on the exam table.

"Who brought you?" she asked.

"Drove myself."

"With a gash like this?"

"Didn't want to wait for a cab."

"What happened?"

"Cut myself shaving."

She flashed a skeptical smirk. "Maybe you should try a Norelco."

He smiled. Her spunky retort had momentarily taken his mind off the pain in his side. His nose and fat upper lip didn't feel so great either. But the diversion didn't last. The smallest movement of his body brought on a scorching burn in his abdomen.

She placed a clean, white towel over the wound.

"Lie back. Keep pressure on your side and ice your lip and nose—on and off every couple of minutes. I'll call for a surgical resident," she said.

She turned and began to walk out of the cubicle. Then she looked back at Gallagher with a parting shot.

"If you stick to that story about the shaving accident, I'll tell the doctor to just have you bite on a bullet while he's placing the stitches."

Gallagher gave her a thumbs up, acknowledging the good comeback. She winked as she pulled back the curtain and left the cubicle.

Within seconds, another nurse came in and placed a blood pressure cuff on his right arm.

"Just need your vitals, Mr. Gallagher," she said.

Good looking, but she has a pasty complexion that matches her lab coat. Is she Irish?

He glanced at the identification tag attached to her belt. He couldn't pick up her name. He decided not to ask.

The nurse never cracked a smile as she quickly recorded his temperature, pulse, and blood pressure.

Then she nodded and said, "Very good."

She was nice enough, but Nurse Number One had it all over her. The personality of this second nurse needed an injection of something.

Or had she seen so many knife wounds that she had become blasé around trauma victims?

"The doctor also wants some blood for a lab work-up.

Which arm do you prefer?" she asked.

"Either one. Doesn't matter."

She held out her hands, palms up, and raised her shoulders. She gave him a puzzled look—almost annoyed at his indecision. Gallagher got the message and extended his right arm toward her.

She tied a rubber tourniquet around his arm and drew a vial of blood. She may have been dull, but she was adept at her craft. When the vial filled, she placed a Band-Aid over the needle site and undid the tourniquet with a flip of her fingers.

"The doctor should be in soon," she said as she pulled back the curtain and left the cubicle with the vial of blood and his chart.

Gallagher waited on the exam table for at least ten more minutes. The white towel gradually turned pink near the wound. The flow of blood had slowed to a trickle. But where was the doctor? Gallagher didn't want to waste more time just lying around in this hospital. His thoughts were focused on finding the man who had tried to kill him—the man who undoubtedly would lead him to Kate and Hayley.

Waiting.

He hated waiting when he knew that he was up against a clock.

Gallagher thought back to the incident in his motel room.

Who had attacked him?

Who ordered it?

The same person or persons who had killed Cindy Kraemer?

What secret are they trying to hide?

His thoughts were interrupted by the sound of the curtain being pulled open. A young man in a scrub suit entered. Nurse Number Two, carrying the chart and a small instrument tray, accompanied him.

"Heard you've got a pretty big cut," he said.

"Easy stitching job for you, Doc," replied Gallagher.

"Shaving accident, huh?"

Gallagher offered a weak smile.

"Yeah. Guess the head nurse filled you in."

"You should know that, in most states, wounds resulting from knife fights or assaults with a knife have to be reported," the doctor said.

"Yes, I know …"

The doctor jumped in. "But Indiana has no such reporting requirement. So feel free to tell me what really happened," he said, as he put on a pair of gloves, lifted the towel away, and leaned down to examine Gallagher's wound.

"Thanks for the heads-up, Doc. But I'll stick to my shaving story and keep the cops out of this."

The doctor forced a smile and shrugged.

"Your choice," he said. "I see from the insurance forms that you're a private investigator."

His eyes remained focused on the wound as he gently approximated the margins of the slash on Gallagher's abdomen.

Gallagher took a deep breath and winced.

"That's right," he said.

"Dangerous job."

"At times."

The doctor motioned to the nurse to open the instrument pack.

"Looks like this wound was made with a pretty sharp razor."

"Yes, very sharp," said Gallagher.

"Luckily, you just gave it a superficial swipe. It's mostly a flesh wound and a little bit of the muscle cut."

"Guess I caught a break when my hand slipped."

"Oh, yes. A little deeper and you could have bled out. I'll give you some local anesthesia and stitch it up."

"So I won't need to bite on that bullet?"

The doctor looked up with a twinkle in his eye.

"No. We'll save that form of anesthesia for the guy who stabbed you."

Chapter 34

Back inside his room at the motel, Gallagher threw the bolt lock on the door and pulled the curtains closed on the windows. He sat on the edge of the bed and unfolded a towel that he had brought in from the trunk of his rental car. Then he lifted out a Smith & Wesson Model 66 .357 Magnum revolver and a folded black knife—the weapons that he had knocked out of the hand of the man who had attacked him earlier that evening. Gallagher had carefully hidden the gun and the knife in the trunk before driving to the hospital. Now he examined them in detail.

The gun had a four-inch barrel and a Hogue black rubber grip. Gallagher flipped open the cylinder and noticed that the serial number on the crane had been obliterated.

Not surprising, he thought.

He knew it was common for criminals to remove the serial number from a gun in order to make it more difficult to trace. But Gallagher also knew that S & W 66s had a second serial number on the base of the frame that was often not visible under the grip.

Gallagher took out the small pen knife that he always carried in his pants pocket. He removed the screw at the bottom of the grip and teased the grip back and forth until he was able to slide it off the handle. The serial number at the base of the frame had been untouched. He grabbed a pen from the nightstand by the bed and jotted the number onto a piece of notepaper.

The knife was a folded, six-inch Cold Steel Ti-Lite with a black Zytel handle and a razor-sharp edge—the tip as sharp as a needle. Gallagher understood why it was so easy for the perp to have carved up his skin with one quick swipe. He also presumed the original intent had been to kill him without using a gun. Better to not attract attention with the sound of a gunshot. But the killer's plans had evidently changed when Gallagher knocked the knife from his hand.

Gallagher leaned back on the bed and thought for a few seconds. Then he reached for his phone, retrieved a name from his contacts list, and pressed the number. A man answered.

"Hey, Paco," said Gallagher.

A brief hesitation and then a response.

"You've reached Francisco Garces. Only my friends call me Paco."

"I am a friend—in fact, an old one."

"Who is this?"

"Gallagher."

"Gallagher? Ha! I haven't heard from you in ages. Why are you calling me so late at night?"

"I need a favor, Paco."

"A favor? Did you forget that I still work for the Boston PD and that you no longer work for the Boston PD?"

Gallagher laughed.

"No, Paco. I haven't forgotten."

"In fact," Paco continued, "there are some cops around here that wish you never worked for the Boston PD."

"I know that, too. But you and I know they're way off base. I never did anything wrong."

"That's your version, my friend."

"If I hadn't broken down that door, Bobby Slater might have killed that girl."

"Did you forget that you didn't have a warrant?"

"No, but I had no choice."

"And then the girl wouldn't testify against him! Worse yet, the evidence in that apartment couldn't be used in his trial because you broke in without a warrant. So Bobby Slater walked—skated away scot-free. He's a bad ass, man."

"I know."

"A lot of cops think he was behind the murder of a detective working undercover."

"You don't have to remind me. If I could change what happened, you know I would."

A long pause. Paco chuckled.

"Hey—I'm just bustin' your chops. You know how it is around here."

"Hasn't changed."

"Right or wrong, some of these guys still hold a grudge. If I do something for you, it's gotta be on the QT. Just between us."

"Don't worry."

"What kind of favor do you need?"

"Are you still working in the Crime Lab?"

"Of course. I got off detail for good about three years ago."

"Alright. I need you to trace a gun for me."

"What kind of gun?"

"S & W 66 .357."

A deep exhale.

"Hmmph. The old stand-by. Where'd you get it?"

"Someone tried to kill me with it."

"Oooh. Sounds like you're still living on the edge, man. You got a serial number on that piece?"

"Yes. The number under the cylinder was obliterated. But whoever ground it off didn't realize that there was a second number on the frame under the grip."

"No one ever accused these guys of being brilliant. Okay, let's have it."

Gallagher slowly recited the serial number and then repeated it to make sure there was no mistake.

"Okay," said Paco. "I'll try to run it down tomorrow morning. I'll call you when I've got something."

"Thanks, Paco.

"No problem, man."

"Hey, Paco—"

"Yeah?"

"The sooner the better."

"What else is new? Never known a detective who said I could just take my time."

Gallagher smiled. The phone clicked before he could say another word.

Chapter 35

Norman Kraemer backed his wheelchair away from the front door and slowly pulled it open. Gallagher stood at the doorway holding a brown paper bag in his hand. Norman looked up at Gallagher's puffy, half-closed eyes, swollen upper lip and the dried blood around his nose.

"Jeez! What the hell happened to you?" asked Norman.

"Just had a little run-in with a guy hiding out in my motel room," said Gallagher.

He reached out and handed the bag to Norman.

"A present for you," he said.

"I wondered why you were so damn late."

"Sorry. Got here as fast as I could."

"Good thing. I'm dyin' for a beer."

Gallagher walked in. Taking careful steps, he worked his way toward the living room. Then he gently eased his body down onto the faded brown couch and leaned his head back on a cushion. Norman grabbed a bottle from the six-pack and twisted off the cap, all the while observing Gallagher's labored movements. He downed a few large gulps of beer and then maneuvered his wheelchair to the front of the couch.

"Little run-in, huh?" said Norman.

"Whatever."

Gallagher took in a deep breath and winced. His eyes remained half-closed as he looked up at the ceiling.

"The guy tried to kill you?" asked Norman.

"I believe that was the intent."

"How?"

"He started out with a knife and then went for his gun."

"Ho-lee shit!" said Norman.

Then he looked down at Gallagher's right hand that was held firmly against his side.

"You got stabbed?" he asked.

"More of a slice."

"How bad?"

"Twenty-five stitches worth."

"Hope you killed the bastard."

"I tried, but he got away. But I ended up with both of his weapons."

"Now what?"

"I'm waiting for some help from a friend in forensics. Maybe I can get an ID on the gun."

"Doubt it. Probably stolen."

"You're probably right. Gotta hope for a break."

"You want a beer?"

"Better not."

Norman took another long swallow.

"You sure? Might ease some of the pain," he said.

"No. I'll live vicariously watching you have a few."

Norman paused for a few seconds.

"Any idea who tried to kill you?"

"I don't know. But I've got a few theories. Remember that unmarked car your brother told you about?"

"Yeah?"

"An unmarked police car followed me today after I left the animal hospital. He tried to stay far enough behind me, but I spotted him anyway. He turned off on another road when I got close to the motel. Once he knew where I was going—guess he decided to call it a night."

"Why are the cops followin' you?"

"It's the sheriff's office. They've got the unmarked cars."

"They should be lookin' for Kate and Hayley. Why the hell are they hasslin' you?"

"They're trying to hide something. I must be getting close to the answer, so they're keeping an eye on me. Somehow your brother—Cindy—Kate—Hayley—they all got caught in the middle of it."

"The guy that attacked you—think you were set up by someone in the sheriff's office?"

"Maybe."

Norman put his empty bottle of beer on a side table and reached into the bag for another.

"Whattya' gonna do?" he asked, as he twisted off the cap.

"You said you knew a guy who used to work there and had some problems and left his job."

"Yeah. Marty Homan."

"Yes, that's the name. Any chance I could speak to him?"

"Not really."

"Why?"

"Long time since I talked to him. After I spoke to you today, I decided to give him a call. His wife gave me the news."

"News?"

"Marty Homan is no longer with us."

Chapter 36

The sound of the marimba chime from his cell phone pulled Gallagher awake out of a deep sleep. He opened his eyes and looked around, trying to get a grasp on his location. His body ached. He blinked a few times to clear his foggy vision and bring the room into focus.

Right! Norman's house. I'm still on the couch. Must have slept here all night.

Norman was nowhere in sight, but snoring as loud as a freight train poured out from the rear bedroom. Six empty beer bottles—lined up on the table to the side of the couch—spoke volumes about how Norman had ended his night.

Gallagher slid the answer key to the right and held the phone up to his ear. He coughed to clear his throat.

"Hello," he said.

"Hey, man. You gave me a job—then you take five rings to answer the phone? What's up with that?"

"Sorry, Paco. I'm a bit out of it. Had a rough night."

"Guess so."

"What time is it?"

"Eight-thirty in Boston."

Gallagher rubbed his eyes and yawned. He desperately needed a cup of coffee.

"Did you come up with anything on that gun?" he asked.

"Yeah. We're hooked into the gun-registry program at ATF. You can get really fast results on a serial number."

Gallagher leaned forward and listened intently. The cobwebs had begun to clear away.

Paco continued, "The gun is registered to a man named David Cooper out of Lafayette, Indiana."

"Cooper?"

"Yeah, that's it. Sound familiar?"

"No. But my mind is pretty messed up right now, so go easy on the trivia tests."

"Cooper's the guy who walked into a police station two years ago and started shooting. Made the national news. Wounded a few cops but fortunately no one died. He was tackled before he had a chance to put the gun to his own head. Convicted a year later of attempted murder of a police officer. Now serving life in an Indiana state prison."

Gallagher remained quiet as he listened and digested all of the details of Paco's story. Then he broke in with his own conclusion.

"So, the police confiscated his gun."

Paco laughed.

"Right on, man! See that? Your mind's not so messed up after all."

Gallagher let the laughter die down. He waited a few seconds before pushing for more details.

"And then—?"

Paco took the hint and continued.

"I checked with a source out there. All confiscated weapons and contraband are turned over to the county sheriff for storage until the trial is over. The weapons are destroyed when the case is settled."

"But obviously not this weapon."

"Right again, Mister Private Eye. That perp who tried to kill you got his gun from the sheriff's office. Had to be."

"And they obliterated the serial number?"

"Yeah, that usually avoids the trace. But somebody screwed up and didn't know that the 66 .357 has the serial number in two places."

"My lucky day, I guess."

"No way, man. Your lucky day was when that perp who tried to kill you missed his mark!"

"Guess you're right."

Gallagher listened for a few more seconds as Paco laughed at his own joke.

"Anything else?" he asked.

Paco's tone turned serious again.

"No. That's about all I have. This is pretty common. A lot of bad guys get their guns from the cops. They're supposed to grind them up in those scissors machines and then sell the scrap metal. But instead, they throw some cheap wrenches into the machine, rub out the serial numbers on the guns, and 'Ooo-la-lah'—they make some cash on the side when they sell the gun. And nobody knows the difference."

"Thanks, Paco. You've been a big help."

"No problem. But—" A long pause. "Hey—Gallagher?"

"Yes?"

"Sounds like someone out there is really out to get you. Maybe you need some backup. Want me to make a few calls?"

"No. I'm alright, Paco. I'm better off handling this one all by myself."

Chapter 37

The ride to Eileen Homan's house took nearly thirty minutes. Gallagher had roused Norman from a deep sleep and convinced him to call Marty's widow to request a brief meeting that morning. She had reluctantly agreed.

"After all," she had said, "How can I help? Marty never talked much about his job with the sheriff's office."

Norman insisted that he should drive his van; Gallagher sat in the front passenger seat.

"You're okay to drive?" asked Gallagher.

"Of course," said Norman.

"You had a lot to drink last night."

Norman gave him a look.

"Yeah? And last night you had a lot of stitches."

Gallagher smiled.

Hard to argue with that sort of logic.

He looked at himself in the vanity mirror on the visor. Eyes not as puffy; nose less swollen; lip near normal. More bruised than battered.

But he desperately needed a shave.

No wonder that nurse didn't believe him.

After a few minutes, Gallagher looked over at Norman.

"Know anything more about Marty's death?"

"Only what she told me when I first called. She said Marty took his own life."

"Was he a guy who got depressed?"

"Not Marty. Never figured that he'd be suicidal. But he was a Gulf War vet—" he said, trailing off.

"Gulf War Syndrome?"

Norman nodded.

"We went through hell over there. A fuckin' toxic swamp. You came home all screwed up. Headaches, rashes, breathin' problems—all kinds of shit. Then you'd remember watchin' some of your buddies gettin' blown up. Depressed? It's easy to get depressed when you go through that. Kinda' creeps up on some guys. Look at me—came home paralyzed—couldn't get a real job—my marriage fell apart. Now I've lost my brother— the only person who was always on my side. These past few weeks—sometimes even I think there's not much to live for."

Gallagher studied the pain on Norman's face while he spoke. A few uneasy moments passed. Did he have more to say? Norman just stared straight ahead. The ever-present rage had re-surfaced.

Finally, Gallagher responded.

"But you're helping me to find Kate and Hayley. And to find out who killed Cindy. Your brother is depending on you; I'm depending on you. You're the only person out here I can trust. That's huge, Norman."

Norman glanced over.

"I know," he said. "It's the only thing that keeps me goin'."

He swallowed hard. His lower lip quivered and his eyes had become misty. He quickly turned his head away, not wanting Gallagher to see his response.

Gallagher understood. When you've got a burn inside, you can never get away from it.

An air of desperation hung over them.

They drove in silence the rest of the way.

Chapter 38

Eileen Homan pushed a few wisps of gray hair away from her forehead and slid forward to the edge of her seat on an armchair in the family room. Gallagher sat on a small couch across from her. Norman had wheeled himself to the doorway where he looked on quietly.

Eileen wore a pair of jeans and a faded red sweatshirt with an Indiana University logo. Despite the color of her hair, she had a young face—smooth skin, no wrinkles—and beautiful blue eyes. Gallagher estimated her age as early fifties.

She clenched her hands together tightly and rested them on her knees.

"Excuse me for being a little nervous. It's always hard to talk about Marty. It's been nearly nine months. Everyone tells me it's time to move on. It's not that easy."

She briefly made eye contact with Gallagher and then abruptly looked away.

He noticed her clenched hands—almost wringing the life out of them—and the wedding band still on her ring finger.

Yes, not so easy to move on, he thought. *I know the feeling.*

Gallagher tried to ease the tension.

"I'm sorry about your loss," he said. "But please, we don't mean to intrude or cause you any discomfort."

She perked up, shook her head quickly, and bit her lower lip.

"It's okay. I'll be fine."

"I believe Norman gave you a little background about our visit."

"Yes."

She looked over at Norman and smiled.

"He said you were a private investigator. Your ex-wife and Norman's little niece are missing. I saw the Amber Alert on TV the other day. That's just terrible. I know the story's been all over the news. Isn't the sheriff's office handling it?"

"Yes. But I have a few issues with them. I'm hoping you may be able to help."

"Me?"

"Yes."

"In what way?"

"Tell me. Why did Marty leave his job with the sheriff's department?"

She took a deep breath and gave a half-smile, almost embarrassed. "Well, he didn't leave on his own."

"What happened?"

"They fired him."

"Why?"

"They said he wasn't a team player; that he asked too many questions that were none of his business and weren't part of his responsibilities."

Gallagher looked puzzled.

"What exactly was Marty's job with the sheriff?" he asked.

"He was a property clerk."

"In the evidence room?"

"Yes. When the deputies made an arrest and confiscated guns or drugs—whatever—they had to be held in the evidence room until the trial was over."

"Was Marty in charge?"

"In charge?"

"I mean, was he the head property clerk?"

"No. He was one of the assistants to the head. But he was full-time and worked there for almost two years."

"Then, what was the problem? What happened to get him fired?"

"I don't know all of the details, but some of the items confiscated were large. You know—bulky boxes or oversized bags—especially when there were huge quantities of drugs from a big bust."

She held her hands apart widely to emphasize her point. Then she continued.

"There wasn't enough space in the evidence-room lockers, so most of that stuff had to be stored off-site in a secure storage facility."

She stopped to take a sip of water. Gallagher waited for more information; it wasn't coming. So he urged her to refocus and continue the story.

"And—?" he asked.

"Oh, yes. Sorry," she said, shaking her head. "Part of Marty's job was to take inventory. He began to notice a few problems in the storage facility."

"Items missing?"

"Not so much missing. 'Substituted' might be a better word."

"What do you mean?"

"Well, one of the drug cases went to court, and the guys they arrested were found guilty. So, with the trial being over, the confiscated drugs were ordered to be destroyed by the sheriff's department. Marty happened to check some of the bags before they were taken to the incinerator."

"Substitution—right?"

"Yes. They had white powder inside, but it wasn't cocaine."

"So what did he do?"

"He was really bothered by the whole thing. The storage facility was supposed to be very secure. You needed two security codes to disarm the alarm and get inside. So, Marty felt there had been a definite breach of security—an inside job."

"Did he report it?"

"Yes. He spoke to his boss. But nothing happened. He told Marty he must have been mistaken."

"I'll bet Marty didn't buy that story."

"Right. He didn't say much to his boss, but he began to quietly check on the inventory in that off-site storage area."

"More substitution?"

"Some of the bags were filled with corn starch instead of cocaine. And some of the guns were missing."

"Guns?"

"Yes. Another trial ended, and several guns were ordered to be destroyed, but when Marty got to the storage locker, the guns were already gone."

"Did he try reporting it again?"

"Yes. His boss said he had taken care of the guns himself and just forgot to make an entry in the log."

"I have a feeling Marty didn't buy that story either."

"No, he didn't. But things really went downhill after that. The officers and deputies were always nice to him, but his boss in the evidence room—that was another story. Really gave Marty a hard time. Changed his hours. Told him he was insubordinate. Then they came up with a new job description that kept him in the main evidence room. Marty no longer had the access codes to the storage facility. A couple of months later, they let him go. They said it was because of budgetary cuts."

"Didn't he file a grievance?"

"Oh, yeah. But it never went anywhere. Not much you can do when you're low man on the totem pole."

"What happened after he got fired?"

"It wasn't easy for him. We had enough money from my job and his unemployment checks to get by. But the whole thing just ate at him—he couldn't let it go."

"So what did he do?"

"He said he was going to the newspapers. To break the story wide open. Create demand for a full investigation. I tried to talk him out of it. I said it was just going to cause us a lot of trouble and could even be dangerous. Besides, what was the point? What would he get out of it? We got into some pretty heated arguments. In fact, it was the start of some hard times in our marriage. Things weren't very good at the end."

She put her hand up to her mouth and looked away.

Her eyes welled up with tears.

"I'm sorry," said Gallagher. "Do you need a minute?"

She inhaled, threw her head back and looked up at the ceiling. She reached over for a tissue and wiped away a tear.

"No. I'm okay. Just once in a while …" she said, as her voice trailed off.

Gallagher waited. He looked over at Norman who shook his head and gave a quick shrug.

Eileen crossed her legs and took another deep breath.

"Really, I'm alright. Is there anything else?"

"If you don't mind—" He paused, giving her time to respond.

"Sure. It's okay."

"Did Marty ever carry out his plan?" Gallagher asked.

"No. At least not that I know of. He just stopped talking to me about the whole thing."

"That was it?"

"No. Wish I could say it was. Then that terrible day. He left the house in the morning. He was acting so strange. Sort of preoccupied. Wouldn't talk much at breakfast. Said he had a meeting. But he never came home. I got the call that afternoon."

"Call? From whom?"

"The county sheriff's department. They found his body at the bottom of the quarry. They said he left the motor of his car running and jumped."

"What about the meeting he was supposed to have?"

"His belongings were returned to me with his cell phone. I checked the numbers he called that day. One of the calls was to a newspaper reporter for the *Lafayette Eagle-Tribune*. I called and spoke to him for quite a while. He was a very nice man. He said Marty had called him to arrange a meeting at his office but never showed up. I turned the information over to the police, and they questioned him about his story. They got back to me and said everything checked out. All the evidence, including the autopsy, pointed to nothing but a suicide."

"When Marty called this reporter, do you know if he told him about the missing contraband from the evidence room?"

"The reporter said Marty never indicated why he wanted to see him. Just said it was something that had to do with the sheriff's office."

"Do you have the reporter's name?"

"Of course. I could never forget it. His name is Gar Kearney."

Chapter 39

B ack in Norman's van, Gallagher stared out the window. This search totally consumed him—every minute, every second. He'd never rest until he found Kate and Hayley and the story behind the deaths of everyone associated with the kidnapping and murders.

He pressed a number into the keypad of his cell.

Phyllis Sax answered.

"Hate to bother you, Phyllis, but I'm running out of time here. Were you able to get a trace on those plates?"

"I was just about to call you. How did you know?"

"Must be ESP."

She laughed.

Gallagher moved right to the basics.

"Okay, what've you got?" he asked.

"The truck is a 2003 Tacoma, registered to a business in Kokomo, Indiana. It's named Sawmill River Farms. I looked it up for you. They sell miniature horses."

"Sawmill River Farms?"

"That's right. I also checked out their website. Those miniature horses are adorable."

"SRF," Gallagher whispered.

That's it, but he was talking to himself.

"What was that?" asked Phyllis.

"Oh—nothing," he said, as he tried to recover from his distracted thoughts. "Just repeated the initials to myself."

"Why? Those initials mean something?"

"More than you can imagine."

"Okay."

"Hey, Phyllis?" He snapped back to reality. "You're the best! Can't thank you enough. This is the information I needed. I'll explain it all when I get back to Boston."

Gallagher pressed "End" and looked over to Norman.

"How far to Kokomo from your house?"

"Kokomo? Maybe forty-five minutes north from my place."

"How fast can you get me to my car?"

Norman gave him a quizzical look.

"If we head up that way from here, it's a bit closer."

"Sorry, Norman. This is not a job for you, my friend. You've been really great, but this could get very dangerous. I don't want you to get hurt. Besides, I need something from my car."

Norman paused for a few seconds. He stared straight ahead at the road. Then he turned back to Gallagher with a half-smile—a knowing smile.

"Your gun, right?"

Gallagher said nothing, and gave Norman a deadpan look.

Norman looked back with a mischievous sparkle in his eyes. His face lit up with a wide smile. Then he broke into an outright laugh.

He twisted the handle of the accelerator sharply forward.

The van immediately picked up speed and moved into the left lane, passing one vehicle after another.

"Hold on, bro'," said Norman excitedly. "You're on your way!"

Chapter 40

"Gar Kearney," said the voice answering the phone.

"Gar—it's Gallagher."

"Hey, I'm glad you called. I've been wondering about you."

"Wondering? In what way?"

"Just interested to see if you have any new information about the guy who brought that dog to the animal hospital."

"No. Nothing new," said Gallagher.

It was an outright lie, but why reveal all the cards in his hand? Instead, Gallagher pushed for more information.

"What about Sanchez? Did you speak to him?" Gallagher asked.

"Left a message. Never got back to me."

"Try him again."

"Okay, I will."

"Does the name Marty Homan mean anything to you?"

A long pause.

"Marty Homan?"

"Yes. Know him?"

"Sure. He's the guy who jumped off the bridge by the Quarry. He called me—oh—maybe nine or ten months ago to arrange a meeting at my office. But he never showed up. Wish I could have talked to him before he decided to end it all. He said there were some issues at the sheriff's office but didn't give me any more than that. Turned out to be a tease with a tragic ending."

"I met his wife today."

"Really? Nice lady. Felt awful for her. Seems like the guy became depressed after he got fired and never snapped out of it. I did some interviews with the other clerks in the evidence room where he worked. Guess he wasn't very popular there— sort of a moody type. They said it was difficult to work with him. I could never come up with anything that even gave a hint of impropriety."

"Ever discuss it with Sanchez?"

"In fact, I did. He hardly knew the guy. Didn't have much to offer. After the autopsy and police reports came out, the case was ruled a suicide and closed."

"Yes, that's what I heard."

"Why the sudden interest? Anything I should know?"

"Not really. His wife is a friend of a friend. Just happened to meet her and heard the story about her husband. When I found out he used to work in the sheriff's office, it got my attention. Then she mentioned that he had called you the morning he took his life."

"Yes he did. Like I said—I wish I had the chance to speak to him and get his story. Maybe there was something there, but, then again, maybe it was his own paranoia. We'll never know."

"Guess not."

"What are you up to?"

"Oh, not much. Had a near death experience last night."

"You what?"

"Yes. Some goon was waiting for me in my motel room."

"What happened?"

"He tried for an appendectomy without the anesthesia."

"My god! Are you alright?"

"Yes. I'm fine."

"Did you report it?"

"Who do you suggest I report it to? The sheriff's office lies to me, and then they send one of their unmarked cars to follow me around. As far as the local cops go, they're ready to throw me in the slammer. Not too many choices for me in Indiana."

"Look—I know some local police. Honest guys. Cops you can trust. Want me to make a call?"

"No. Let it slide. I'll be okay."

"Anything new about Kate and Hayley?"

"No, Gar. Nothing new. I'll be in touch if I come up with anything."

"Well, don't hesitate to call me. I want to get to the bottom of this as much as you do. I'm here to help."

"I know. Thanks, Gar."

Click.

Gallagher continued driving. It was just a few more miles until he should reach Sawmill River Farms.

Chapter 41

12:48 pm

Gar Kearney looked at his watch.

He finished his cup of coffee, got up from the table, and walked over to a large "Arrivals" monitor on the wall. He scanned down the list until he reached "Boston – Flight 921—Status – In."

Gar walked to the arrival corridor and stood at the end of the walkway leading from the arrival gates. While he waited, he took out a black Sharpie marking pen and quickly scribbled the name "Winston" on a piece of white cardboard. He stood next to the rope and held the sign in front of his waist in the manner of a limo driver waiting for his fare.

A few minutes passed.

A long line of passengers began to make their way up the inclined walkway pulling their carry-on baggage. Several people glanced at Kearney's sign and then looked away.

Finally, a large man approached.

"Mr. Kearney?" he asked.

"Yes—Matt?" Gar replied.

Matt Winston extended his hand.

"Right. Thanks for offering to pick me up. I really appreciate it," said Matt.

"No problem. Newspaper reporters are always happy to meet new sources. I'm anxious to hear what you have to say."

The two men walked together toward the exit. Gar looked up at the much taller young man.

"Were you an athlete?" Gar asked.

"Yeah. Played some football."

"College?"

"And pro."

"Really? That's great. Which team?"

"Patriots. I was a linebacker."

"Guess I should have recognized your name."

"It's alright—I wasn't much of a star."

They kept walking.

"Have any other luggage?" asked Gar.

"Just one bag."

"Baggage claim is down this way," Gar said as he pointed to an escalator on the right.

"So, tell me again, how did you find out about me?" Gar asked.

"I Googled Kate's name before I left Boston. Your story in the newspaper popped up. So I decided to give you a call."

"And you said you had some information that might make the next installment pretty interesting?"

"Oh, yes, Mr. Kearney. I have a lot to tell you."

Matt stopped and turned to face Gar head on. He glared down into the reporter's eyes.

"And when I'm through, I'm going to expect a lot from you."

Chapter 42

Gallagher slowed down as he reached the entrance to Sawmill River Farms. He studied the sign about the farm's championship miniature horses.

He turned in and followed the one-lane road toward a large, red barn in the distance. Along the way, he passed several workers who were repairing a section of white fence that lined the road. The fence extended into gated sections of pasture where more than a dozen miniature horses grazed on the grass. The workers hardly noticed him as they glanced up at his passing car and then resumed their work.

Gallagher reached the barn and pulled into a space marked "Visitor Parking." He got out of his car and looked around. He could see a large farmhouse nearly a hundred yards away. A black Chevy Tahoe and a small blue pickup truck were parked alongside the barn. His attention was instantly drawn to the truck—a Toyota Tacoma bearing the license plate that had been seen at the Clarkson Animal Hospital—the same license plate that Phyllis had traced to this location.

A man approached—short, stocky, with a thick gold necklace around his neck and wearing a baseball-style hat, jeans, and a blue shirt with a logo on the sleeve—*SRF*. He looked up at Gallagher and gave a wide, gap-toothed smile.

"Welcome to Sawmill River Farms," he said.

"Beautiful animals you have here," said Gallagher.

"Thanks. We're quite proud of 'em."

The smile quickly vanished. He cast a suspicious eye at Gallagher.

Does he know who I am? Gallagher wondered.

"I'm the foreman," the man said. "How can I help you?"

"Might be interested in buying one of your horses. What do they cost?"

"All depends. Geldings run about a thousand or more. Mares start at twenty-five hundred. Show stallions can be as much as fifty thousand."

"Fifty thousand! Whew! That's a lot of money. Never expected them to be that expensive. Think I'd be in the market for one of the lower-priced horses. It's for an aunt who lives in a country home and used to ride. She really loves horses."

"They make great companions."

"She lives back East. Do you ship that far?"

"No problem. We ship anywhere."

Gallagher looked over toward the farmhouse.

"Beautiful home. You live there?"

The foreman stepped back. His eyes narrowed.

"No that's the owner's house."

His responses had become measured and calculated.

"Is he around?"

"No. If you want to buy a horse, you deal with me."

"No offense intended, but I'd prefer to speak to the owner."

Now more annoyed, the man glared out at Gallagher.

"That's not possible. The owner is not expected back for quite a while. He put me in charge."

"You've got a beautiful property here. Are there more fields in the back where the horses graze?"

The foreman ignored the question and responded with a snarl.

"The only horses for sale are right here."

"That's too bad. I was hoping for a larger selection."

The foreman stepped forward.

"What did you say your name was?"

"I didn't."

"Look—maybe you've asked enough questions and should be gettin' on your way."

Another man walked out from the entrance to the barn—taller, muscular, and more rugged than the foreman. He had some bruises on his face. He placed his hands on his hips and stared at Gallagher.

An aggressive posture.

The guy appeared to be more than just a casual observer.

The men working on the fence had also put their tools down and looked at the developing confrontation.

Reinforcements, for sure.

Gallagher took a quick inventory—at least five against one. No guns visible but some of the opposition possibly were armed.

Not good odds.

"Well, I appreciate the information," he said. "I'll check with my aunt and get back to you."

He spun to his left and walked toward his car.

For a split second, he questioned his decision to turn his back on these guys.

But nothing happened.

He almost wished it had. There was nothing he'd rather do than beat the crap out of that wise-ass little foreman.

Gallagher got into his car and turned the ignition.

The men stood and watched as he drove away.

Chapter 43

Nighttime

Gallagher carefully picked his way through the forest that bordered the horse farm. He carried a pen flashlight in his pocket but didn't dare use it on his approach.

Not a good time to attract unwanted attention.

Instead, he relied upon the dim moonlight to guide him around the dead tree limbs, rocks, and underbrush that lined the floor of the woods.

One misstep and a broken ankle would put an end to the night and perhaps end his chance to find Kate and Hayley.

He finally caught sight of the white fence that stretched along the right side of the road all the way back to the barn. As he followed the fence line, he could see a single light near the barn that illuminated the main door and parking area.

There were no cars or vehicles to be seen by the barn.

Gallagher moved slowly through the trees on the left side of the entrance road. The farmhouse loomed ahead to the far left of the barn. It was in total darkness—not an outside light or a lamp in a window.

Again, not a car in sight.

Where is everyone?

Do they leave these horses completely unattended at night?

A loud cracking noise startled him as he stepped awkwardly on a dead limb that snapped under his foot. He lost his balance and fell to the ground. He felt a tear in the stitches and grabbed at his side.

Moisture.

Probably blood. No time to dwell on it.

He remained crouched on the ground for a minute. He listened, but heard nothing—no movement or sounds from the barn or farmhouse.

Still no lights.

Still safe.

The entire setting remained eerily quiet.

He got to his feet and continued his slow trek toward the farmhouse.

Could Kate and Hayley be held there? In the darkness?

He reached the front steps. No sign of life. The furniture on the front porch remained in the same position as he had seen it when he drove out in the afternoon. Gallagher moved around to the side of the house and peered in through a window.

Darkness.

No sign of life.

He walked to the back of the farmhouse.

Still nothing.

Only the sounds of nature penetrated the night air as the grinding and chirping of the crickets and cicadas reverberated from the woods.

Gallagher turned to his left and could just make out a dark dirt road leading back from the farmhouse. The road extended deeper into the woods and was lined by tall maple and birch trees—so tall that virtually none of the dim moonlight reached the road.

What's back there?

He walked along the edge of the dirt road trying to remain inconspicuous while at the same time avoiding the hazard of the ditch and sudden drop-off. The breeze picked up and whistled through the dense layer of trees.

Suddenly, a light from behind.

A car coming?

He ducked down to the side of the road and lay flat on his stomach. The ditch had become a friendly haven.

He waited.

No more light.

No sounds.

Was that a car from the main road that just got lost and turned around?

He waited longer to be sure.

His heart pounded.

Still no lights. Just the sounds of Mother Nature.

He crawled to his feet and looked all around.

No one in sight.

He continued walking down the dirt road.

In the distance—perhaps fifty yards away and barely visible in the dim moonlight—he could see a wooden structure.

A small house.

Large boulders marked the end of the road. No passage beyond this point. A dead end.

The house was set back from the road by more than thirty feet. Completely out of view from the farmhouse or barn.

The windows were boarded up with plywood, and the clapboards were dry—nearly rotting.

Was this house abandoned? Or perhaps a great place to hide someone?

He moved closer, taking cautious steps.

He approached the side of the little house and pressed his ear against the outside wall. Not a sound from within

He turned and looked back down the dirt road to make sure that no one had followed him. Then, he moved toward the front door. A heavy-gauged padlock secured the entrance.

Why would a lock be needed here? What could be of value in a run-down place like this? Unless someone wanted to keep the occupants from getting out?

He reached into his pocket and removed his hook pick—an essential tool that he always carried in the event that access was denied but completely necessary.

He worked the pick into the lock and twisted it slightly.

The lock released with a click.

He removed the lock and opened the latch.

He gently pushed the door open.

Not a sound inside.

Total darkness.

He reached into his pocket for the small pen flashlight. The light was a risk, but he had no choice. He had to see what was in this cabin.

He flipped on the flashlight.

An opened box of Animal Crackers and a partially-filled glass of milk rested on a small table in front of a threadbare couch. He picked up the glass. The milk was lukewarm, but fresh. He stepped into the kitchen and pulled the refrigerator door open. There was orange juice, a half-gallon container of milk, assorted fruit, and other odds and ends of leftovers. The expiration date on the container of milk had two weeks remaining.

He found assorted groceries in the cabinets.

Someone is living here.

He walked toward the bedroom.

The floorboards creaked—the only sounds that could be heard in this little house.

He reached the bedroom door, almost afraid of what he might find inside, and gently pushed the door open and flashed his light on the bed.

Empty.

He saw a child's pair of sneakers scattered on the floor, and a woman's sweater thrown across the bed.

He stepped further into the bedroom.

There were two toothbrushes in the tiny bathroom—one child, one adult and both moist.

His heart sank.

Kate and Hayley had been here.

Gallagher turned and looked all around. No other rooms to search.

What next?

An uneasy feeling turned his gut into knots.

Kate and Hayley were still missing.

Chapter 44

Gallagher flipped off the flashlight and moved toward the front door of the house. A hint of dim moonlight glimmered through the open door and slightly illuminated the main room. He looked back, over his shoulder, for one last look inside. Did he miss anything?

He was startled by a clicking noise from outside.

What's that?

He turned to look, and with his eyes now well-adjusted to the darkness, he could see the figure of a man standing in front of him on the edge of the road.

His first instinct was to bolt and seek cover, but then Gallagher froze.

The man was pointing a gun directly at him—a man that Gallagher recognized, even in the darkness.

"Not surprised to see you here, Gar."

"Don't make a move, Gallagher."

"It must be getting easy for you to kill these days, Gar. You've had lots of practice."

"Just be quiet and keep your hands where I can see them."

"Is this how you handled Marty Homan before you pushed

him off that ledge at the quarry?"

"He was a foolish man that stuck his nose where it didn't belong. We had to keep him quiet before he went to another newspaper."

"And then you got a call from Cindy Kraemer, didn't you?"

"Shut up!"

"What a lucky break. Huh, Gar?"

"Stop it!"

"Cindy couldn't get any satisfaction from the sheriff's office so she called the most famous investigative reporter in Indiana. Someone who could break the story of corruption in the sheriff's office wide open—none other than Gar Kearney."

"That's enough or I'll drop you right here."

"No, Gar. That's not your style. The cops need to find the victim somewhere where it looks like an accident. You tried to make it look like Cindy's car crashed and burned, but there wasn't enough gasoline in the car to completely burn her body. You didn't figure on the autopsy report showing that she was dead before you pushed her car off the road and down that ravine."

"You think you're pretty smart, don't you Gallagher?"

"Smart enough to see through you Gar. What made you hook up with Sanchez and these crooked cops anyway?"

"Why else? You can't make much money working for a small town newspaper. Once I got involved, I got in too deep. I had no choice. If I didn't keep these shipments going, these guys would have eliminated me, too."

"Oh, yeah. The drug runs. And throw in a large collection

of confiscated guns. Untraceable. They're the best kind. Clever idea you had of hiding them in the horse shipments."

"Stop running your mouth, or I'll close it for you."

"And that goon you sent to my room? Would've worked out very nice for you as a 'stab and grab.' Boston private eye mugged in Indiana. A great story for a crime reporter like you."

"You think you've got it all figured out? Well, Mister Private Eye, you just might have brought about your own demise and that of Kate and that little girl. If you hadn't come snooping around here, they would have been released—out of state—safe and sound. But after your little visit to the farm today, I got a call, and we had to move them."

Gallagher stepped forward.

"Where are they?" he asked.

"Somewhere safe—at least for now."

"For now?'

"The little girl will be alright; can't say the same about your 'ex.' She knows too much. Especially after today. You can take the blame for that, Gallagher. Just don't know when to quit, do you?"

Gallagher moved closer.

"You bastard!"

"Another step and you're a dead man."

"You hurt her, and you won't live another day."

"That's something I'm afraid you'll never know."

Gar lifted his gun, taking dead aim at Gallagher.

Gallagher darted quickly to his left.

Taken by surprise, Gar fired wildly.

Bullets blasted into the cabin walls.

Gallagher reached behind to the holster on the back of his belt and retrieved his Glock.

Gar took several steps forward and fired another shot but missed his mark once again. Now at close range he pointed his gun directly at his target about to deliver his last act of violence.

But Gallagher responded too fast and pumped two rapid rounds from his Glock into Gar's chest.

The shots echoed loudly.

Gar's knees buckled. The gun dropped out of his hand. He drew a last gasping breath—a painful groan—and fell to the ground in a wilted heap.

Gallagher rushed over to Gar. He reached down to feel the side of Gar's neck and placed his other hand in front of his mouth.

No pulse. No breathing.

Gar Kearney was dead.

Chapter 45

Gallagher had little time to dwell on the dead body in front of him. The quiet darkness of the farm exploded with the sound of sirens and the glare of flashing blue and red lights. A police bull horn crackled in the distance. A large portable spotlight moved down the entrance road on the back of a truck and lit up the horse barn.

The farm had suddenly come under police siege.

A reaction to the shots fired here?

No.

The activity was completely focused on the horse barn nearly three-hundred yards away.

A man's voice blared through the bull horn. Gallagher could not make out the entire warning message that was broken up by static and the distance to the barn. Several words, however, had been clear—"Surrender ... put down your weapons ..."

Gallagher raced down the dirt road.

A battalion of police cruisers lined the main entrance road leading up to the barn. Two cruisers, labeled Sheriff's Department, were parked parallel to the front of the barn. Several deputies crouched down, taking cover behind the cruisers. Their guns were drawn and aimed at the barn door. A tall officer—over six feet—stood behind one of the cruisers and barked messages through the bull horn.

Is that Captain Sanchez? Yes, Bob Sanchez!

Leading the bust? He should be under arrest!

Gallagher stopped before reaching the crossroad from the farmhouse to the barn. At least twelve sheriff's deputies had completely surrounded the horse barn. Some wore bulletproof vests and SWAT team tactical helmets and carried military-style automatic weapons.

Is this a drug bust or a war?

"Drop your weapons and come out with your hands above your heads. You have no chance to escape. Let the woman and child come out first," said Sanchez.

Woman and child? Kate and Hayley are being held hostage inside that barn!

Instead of walking down the road, Gallagher ran across the field and approached the barn from the left. A young deputy sheriff turned around and spotted him. He raised his automatic weapon and aimed it at Gallagher.

"Stop right there, mister!" he yelled.

Gallagher froze in his tracks.

The deputy approached. His facial muscles clenched with tension. He seemed prepared to empty his magazine into Gallagher's mid-section as he marched toward him.

All at once the deputy's demeanor softened.

He lowered his gun.

"Mr. Gallagher?" he asked.

Shocked that he knew him, Gallagher responded, "Yes. I am."

The deputy offered a half-smile—almost embarrassed by his harsh comportment just seconds earlier.

"Sorry, sir. Didn't recognize you at first. Captain Sanchez told us to be looking out for you. Come over here with me where you'll be safe. The men in that barn are armed and highly dangerous."

Captain Sanchez looking out for me?

The deputy led him to an area behind a cruiser that was parked at a forty-five degree angle to the barn with a direct view of the front doors.

"What's going on here?" asked Gallagher.

"Captain Sanchez ordered a raid on this barn. Several employees from the sheriff's office and two of our deputies were arrested today in a sting operation. There are three men in the barn who conspired with them. They're holding a woman and a little girl hostage. We're trying to get them out of there alive."

Gallagher resisted the urge to move closer—to try to do something to free Kate and Hayley, but there was no possibility. He could only wait for these thugs to make a move, and in the best case, for them to surrender without causing a bloody firefight.

A few agonizing moments passed—silent except for Sanchez's periodic warnings to the men inside the barn, which drew no response.

Gallagher felt gut-wrenching uncertainty as the impasse developed.

A child's piercing cry suddenly broke the silence, sending a chill through Gallagher.

The large door on the right side of the barn swung open.

The deputies crouched down behind the cruisers with their guns resting on the hoods or trunks to support their aim.

Gallagher reached back and removed his Glock from its holster.

"Easy, men," said Sanchez. "Stay in control of your weapons. Let's be very careful here."

Without warning, a steady stream of miniature horses stampeded out of the barn. The entire herd, nearly thirty strong, charged into the semi-circular dirt parking area, spurred on by a series of loud whoops and yells that emanated from within the barn. However, upon confronting the glaring spotlights and the barricade of police vehicles, the frightened animals came to a near screeching halt. Some stumbled and fell, then struggled to regain their footing in the midst of a frenzied turmoil of dust and whinnies. Some of the horses ran in circles—their ears pricked forward in fear. Others darted back and forth as they frantically tried to escape the confined area.

The young deputy looked toward Gallagher. "What the hell …?" he asked as his voice trailed off in confusion.

"Ground cover," said Gallagher.

"Ground cover?"

"They must have an escape vehicle in that barn. They want to be sure you won't be able to shoot the tires out. Those little horses are perfect cover for them."

Next a loud call from the barn.

"We're coming out!" a voice screamed.

A tall, muscular man stepped out from the door clutching Hayley with his left arm—a gun pointed to her head. Gallagher saw it was the same man who had backed up the foreman earlier in the day.

A much shorter man emerged a few seconds later.

The foreman!

He pulled Kate by the arm and joined his accomplice in front of the barn. Kate's hands were tied behind her back. The foreman jammed his gun into Kate's ribcage.

I should have killed this little sonovabitch when I had the chance, thought Gallagher.

The men stood side by side maintaining a death grip on their hostages.

The miniature horses continued to scurry around them.

The foreman yelled to Sanchez.

"We're leaving here now and you're not going to follow. If you do, you'll find one of these two on the side of the highway. If you fire even one shot, we shoot one of them—understand?"

Sanchez held his ground and didn't respond.

The second door on the left opened. A third man stepped out and secured this door in the open position. His eyes darted around wildly as he surveyed the mass of deputies with guns trained on him and his accomplices. Then he nervously back-stepped in retreat toward the inside of the barn.

The guy who attacked me at the motel, thought Gallagher. *Looks like the weak link.*

The foreman scanned the array of sheriff's deputies and

police vehicles blocking the exit roads from the barn. He pointed to the cruiser in front of Gallagher.

"Get that car out of the way now!" he yelled.

"Take it easy, here," said Sanchez. "Let's talk this over."

His voice was calm and reassuring.

"Hey—did you hear me? No delaying tactics," hollered the foreman. "Get that car out of our way or you're going to start seeing blood on the ground."

Sanchez looked over to the young deputy with Gallagher. His face had a resigned look. He motioned backwards with his hand.

"Okay. Move it," he called out.

All attention now focused on the deputy who walked around to the front of his cruiser. He opened the door, hopped into the front seat, and started the engine. The sound of the car caused several of the horses to retreat toward the barn where they joined their excited mates that milled around in a state of confusion.

Before the police car started to move, Gallagher ducked down and slipped off to the left. Staying low to the ground, he made his way through the shadows of the trees to a small door on the side of the barn.

He stood next to the door with his back leaning up against the barn, completely out of the view of the two men holding Kate and Hayley.

He raised his left arm.

Gallagher prepared to fire his Glock if necessary.

He waited for a sound—an indication that a vehicle had

driven out of the barn.

Within seconds, he heard the sound of a motor.

Gallagher pulled the side door of the barn open and dived in. He found himself lying on a straw-covered wooden floor between two horse stalls.

He quickly slid forward in time to see the back of a large, black, Chevy Tahoe as it drove out of the barn. The miniature horses scurried away from the path of the approaching vehicle.

The Chevy Tahoe came to an abrupt stop.

The motor kept running.

The driver jumped out from behind the steering wheel and opened the passenger door behind the driver's seat and then ran back to open the tail-gate for the rear seating area. His head darted side-to-side but he never looked back into the barn.

Gallagher crawled forward along the side of the stalls until he neared the entrance.

The horses milled all around the Tahoe. Several bounded back toward the entrance of the barn. They stopped, as if wondering whether or not to enter. Gallagher stayed low, now using the little horses as his own protective cover.

The driver rushed over to the man holding Hayley and led him toward the rear of the Tahoe. The rear seats were not installed. Gallagher assumed that the tall man planned to merely climb in and lie down in the storage area. He clutched Hayley in his left arm and held his gun toward her head as they walked backwards along the side of the car. She twisted and squirmed and tried to scratch at his face.

Kate screamed, "Please—let her go!"

The gunmen ignored her, and the foreman jammed his gun harder and deeper into Kate's ribs.

Kate struggled to get free, but his grasp was too strong.

Sanchez stepped around to the front of his cruiser. He walked toward the foreman. The miniature horses moved away as he strode forward.

"Let them go. Take me as your hostage if you want," he said.

Sanchez tossed his gun to the ground to prove he was unarmed.

"Come any closer and you're dead!" yelled the foreman.

The two men approaching the rear door of the Tahoe stopped for a second, apparently unsure of the outcome of Sanchez's dramatic move. The driver removed a gun from his rear pocket and now held it in his left hand.

Gallagher stood up.

Both men had their backs to him. Gallagher looked out toward Sanchez. Their eyes met.

If Sanchez was surprised to see him, he never showed it.

Sanchez gave a quick, almost imperceptible nod, but it was an undeniable signal, recognizing that Gallagher had managed to single-handedly outflank the opposition.

Sanchez remained cool and now directed his attention to the two men with Hayley.

"You men back there—consider what you're doing. Put the girl down and drop your weapons."

The men hesitated.

They looked over toward the foreman for help.

"Whaddya' waitin' for? Get in the fuckin' car and get us

outta here," snarled the foreman.

The men backed around the Tahoe, seemingly afraid to take their eyes off the battalion of sheriff's deputies with high-powered weapons trained on them.

The man who held Hayley in his left arm took several side-steps and prepared to crawl into the rear storage area with her. He struggled to contain the young child whose kicking and squirming had become virtually uncontrollable. The driver offered no help and merely slipped slightly to his right, taking refuge behind the rear of the vehicle while continuing to point his gun out toward Sanchez. Finally, in a desperate attempt to control the little girl, the tall man slipped his gun into his rear pocket, and then, using both hands, he lifted Hayley and shoved her into the back of the Tahoe.

The foreman had dragged Kate to the door behind the driver's seat. He tried to pull her into the back seat, but she resisted. He worked one of his legs into the Tahoe and plopped down on the edge of the seat. He pulled violently on her arm and tried to force her into the vehicle.

"Get in or I'll pull the trigger, you bitch," he snarled.

"Go ahead—you'll lose your protection—they'll kill you—you'll get what you deserve."

She gave him a defiant look and continued resisting.

Suddenly, a loud voice bellowed from the entrance to the barn.

"Drop it!" yelled Gallagher.

Startled by the voice behind them, the driver and the taller man turned.

The driver raised his gun and aimed it toward Gallagher.

The taller man reached back for his gun.

Too late.

Gallagher fired two precise shots that struck each man in the chest.

The driver's body slammed back against the Tahoe and dropped to the ground.

The taller man clutched at his chest and slipped down to one knee.

He made another futile attempt to retrieve his gun from his back pocket.

Gallagher ran forward and, using the butt of his Glock, delivered a crushing back-handed blow to the side of the man's head.

The man collapsed to the ground.

Gallagher jumped into the back of the Tahoe on his knees.

He flipped his Glock to his left hand.

"It's okay, Hayley. You're safe now,' he said as he held her gently against the rear divider with his right arm.

Hayley screamed hysterically. Gallagher steadied her body against the divider and tried to calm her.

The foreman had been completely caught off guard by the noise behind the car. He turned his head sharply.

Kate broke out of his grasp and fell to the ground on her back near the rear tire.

Her hands still tied behind her back, she dug her heels into the ground and pushed herself away from the vehicle.

Then she began to roll—over and over, trying to get further

away from the vehicle and out of close range of the foreman's gun.

Frightened by the sound of gunshots, the miniature horses ran wildly away from the barn.

The crush of chaotic activity caused a few of the horses to rear up on their hind legs. Others turned and kicked their legs in a backward direction. Their bodies stumbled and fell into one another as they sought to escape from the confined area in front of the barn.

Kate lay on the ground in the midst of the bedlam, unable to protect her head from the hooves of the horses.

Sanchez recognized the danger and rushed through the herd.

He dove onto the ground and covered Kate's head with his arms and shoulders.

The foreman leaned out of the Tahoe and fired a shot at Sanchez.

The horses bolted away in near terror.

Then another shot, and a cloud of dust exploded from the dirt, but both shots had missed their mark.

Gallagher crawled up on his knees and extended his arm forward.

Now without his hostage, the foreman swung his legs into the Tahoe and slammed the door, trying to shield himself from gunfire from the deputies.

He began to crawl into the front seat in a desperate attempt to escape.

Where was his driver?

He spun around to look toward the rear of the car.

His eyes widened as he saw the muzzle of Gallagher's Glock literally inches from his face.

Gallagher yelled, "Freeze!"

The foreman quickly leaned to the side, but he had no time to escape.

He tried to twist his gun back at Gallagher, but he was too slow.

Gallagher fired twice in rapid succession—the "double tap" all combat shooters are trained in.

Both 9mm bullets struck the foreman squarely in the forehead, and blood and brains splattered across the inside of the windshield and the dashboard of the car.

The foreman's mouth dropped open, his body arched violently toward the front seats, and his gun fell from his hand as his body crumpled to the floor.

The entire sequence had taken less than five seconds.

The small army of deputies moved in on the bloody scene. But they quickly lowered their weapons, realizing that the threat had been eliminated.

All three men were dead.

Chapter 46

Gallagher reached down to lift Hayley out of the Tahoe. He picked her up into his arms.

"You're okay now, sweetheart. Everything's okay," he said as he cradled her close to his body.

He walked around to the side of the vehicle.

Sanchez had already removed the ties from Kate's wrists and had helped her to her feet. Stunned and disoriented, she brushed the dust from her face and clothes.

In a second of near-panic, she looked around and cried, "Hayley?"

In another half-second, a look of bewilderment and joy overcame her.

Gallagher walked closer.

He reached out and handed Hayley over to her.

"Here's your little girl. She's safe now."

Kate took Hayley into her arms. Hayley wrapped herself around Kate's neck and hugged her tightly. Tears streamed down Kate's face as she patted Hayley's back.

She stepped closer to Gallagher and looked into his eyes.

She leaned her head on his chest.

"I prayed for you to come—I knew you would," she said.

He swallowed hard and looked up to the sky. He was nearly overcome by the emotion of seeing her alive, and his eyes began to well up.

"Why didn't you tell me?" he asked.

"I couldn't. I knew how you'd react if you knew a man had raped me. You would have gone after him. You would have killed him. I didn't want to lose you that way."

She pressed her head harder against him.

"No more secrets—I promise."

He placed his arm around her

A chuisle mo chroi," he said.

She lifted her hand to his face.

"*Mo chuisle.*"

He kissed her forehead.

"I'll never leave you again," she said.

He smiled.

"I'll never give you a reason to try."

Chapter 47

The full contingent of deputies took control of the scene and began herding the horses back into the barn. Two young EMTs escorted Kate and Hayley to an ambulance parked at the head of the entrance road.

Captain Sanchez, his face and uniform covered with dirt and debris, approached Gallagher.

"Thanks, Gallagher. Pretty impressive," Sanchez said.

Gallagher gave him a blank look.

"Always shoot that fast?" Sanchez asked.

"Usually faster. But I had a few distractions out here."

Sanchez smiled weakly.

It was an awkward moment.

A crusty older man wearing an EMT uniform that barely contained his barrel chest walked up to Sanchez.

"You okay, Captain?" he asked.

"Yes, Billy. Thanks for checking."

"Must admit, Captain—when I saw you jump down to protect that woman and then heard the gunshots, I had to hold my breath," said the EMT. "I was afraid I'd be haulin' your ass out of here on a gurney."

Sanchez laughed.

"Not today, Billy. Dodged another one."

Gallagher's surprised gaze turned to Sanchez. Their eyes met.

Another awkward moment.

"Sorry—I didn't see everything that happened. I should be thanking you," said Gallagher.

Sanchez shrugged.

"I can move pretty fast myself when I have to."

Gallagher smiled.

"Guess I deserved that. But I still have a lot of questions."

"I'm sure you do," said Sanchez.

He lifted his chin and a confident look came over his face.

"You're probably wondering why I lied to you?"

Gallagher nodded. "Yes. There's no reason to dance around it any longer."

"We'd been tracking the missing contraband from our evidence locker for a while. We found a link between a few of our clerical employees and two of our deputies. They were all meeting with Gar Kearney. You met one of them...Norris—the guy who tried to brush you off. I knew why you were here—to find your ex-wife—but couldn't let you know too much about our investigation for fear you'd let something slip to Gar."

"But, what was the connection to the abduction of Kate and Hayley? How did you tie their disappearance to the missing contraband from your evidence locker?"

"After Don Kraemer's death, we got a few calls from Cindy asking why we hadn't followed up on her husband's claims about a dog attack. I didn't know what she was talking about. We did some research and found a log entry that Don Kraemer had come to the office a few weeks ago to file a report. But the report indicated that Kraemer had filed a mugging incident with no mention of a dog. We checked further. The deputy who filed the report is one of the same guys who had been linked to Gar Kearney.

"He had also told the switchboard that he was following the case and to make sure all calls from Don Kraemer were funneled to him. We asked ourselves—why would this deputy file a phony report? What was it about Don Kraemer that he was trying to hide? When Cindy was found dead along State Road 5, we knew that it was all linked."

"How did this horse farm get involved?"

"The owner and his wife went to Europe to tend to her sick mother. They've been gone for more than six months. They put the foreman in charge. According to the guys we have in custody, Gar knew the owners and hooked up with the foreman. He masterminded the whole thing."

"I figured the drugs and guns were being shipped with the horses," said Gallagher.

"Oh—yeah. You're right about that. They modified the horse trailers with four-inch thick false walls all around the interior and stuffed them with bags of cocaine, heroin, and some guns."

"So that pretty much wraps up your case?"

"Well, we still have to pick up Gar Kearney."

Gallagher hesitated.

He took out his Glock and held it by the barrel. He handed it to Sanchez and pointed back behind the barn.

"You'll find Gar on the road by a small guest house back there. You'll need my gun to verify that I shot him. But he tried to kill me. Your forensic guys will figure out what happened."

Sanchez nodded knowingly.

"You mind coming back to the station with me to fill out a report?"

Kate, holding Hayley, approached.

"Are you okay?" asked Gallagher.

"We're fine …just a bit shaken up."

Sanchez looked at Kate. "Can one of my deputies take you somewhere?"

"The best place now would be Norman's house. Hayley needs to feel safe and be around family."

She looked toward Gallagher.

"We'll wait for you there," she said.

Chapter 48

One hour later

Following nearly two weeks of incredible tension and fear, the solitude of Norman's house was a welcome respite for Kate. She walked out of a small guest bedroom where Hayley was sleeping peacefully. She gently closed the door and smiled at Norman who was in the living room sitting in his wheelchair.

"What a nightmare this has been. Thank God it's over and Hayley is safe," she said.

"That little angel has suffered way too much. And so have you," he answered.

Norman paused for a second, absorbing his thought. Then he exclaimed, "I need a beer," as he motored toward the kitchen.

Kate stood in the middle of the room, stretched back, took a deep breath and exhaled.

A sigh of relief.

The quiet of the room was interrupted by the sound of the doorbell.

Kate turned and looked toward the door.

She hesitated.

Norman called from the kitchen, "I'll get it. Probably the media lookin' for a sound bite."

Kate shrugged. "That's okay. I'll send them away."

Kate walked over to the door and opened it.

Then, she stepped back in shock.

She made a loud gasp.

Her hand reached up and tried to cover her mouth as she saw Matt Winston standing behind the screen door.

Nearly breathless, she exclaimed, "Matt?"

"Finally found you, Kate," he said coldly.

"What are you doing here?"

"I want to see my daughter."

Kate's voice quivered, "How did you find us?"

"I've been doing my own detective work. Got some information from Mr. Kearney at the newspaper. He said he would help me find Hayley and that sooner or later you might turn up here. Haven't been able to reach him all day so I thought I'd take a chance and come here myself."

Then, with a chilling inflection he added, "And look who answers the door."

Kate pressed hard with both arms in an attempt to close the door as she cried out, "Matt, you should go!"

But Matt quickly opened the screen door and forcibly prevented Kate from closing the front door.

"Where's Hayley?" he yelled as he stepped inside toward a retreating Kate.

"Matt, you should leave now," she begged.

Matt became defiant and began pacing toward Kate, crowding her space in an intimidating manner.

His face filled with rage.

"I'm not going anywhere until I see Hayley. She's my daughter and you've kept her from me for three years. You had no right to do that, Kate. She's mine."

Norman heard the commotion and had driven his wheelchair into the room, stopping a short distance away from Matt. He held a handgun and pointed it directly at Matt.

"The lady said you should leave," said Norman coldly.

Matt turned toward Norman and angrily pleaded his case. "You don't understand. Hayley is my daughter and I intend to establish my rightful place in her life."

Unimpressed with his plea, Norman inched a bit closer to Matt and delivered a final warning.

"All I understand is that you better get your ass out of here before I either call the police or pull this trigger."

Matt raised his arms and then dropped them to his side in frustration, seemingly resigned to his fate. He turned toward the door as if leaving, then suddenly made a reverse spin move and lunged toward Norman.

Norman fired his gun wildly but the bullets harmlessly struck the ceiling.

Norman spilled out of his wheelchair and fell to the floor under the force of his much larger and stronger attacker. The gun slid away, out of his reach.

Norman flailed his arms at Matt trying to strike a blow to his face and keep him away from Kate. Matt fended off all of his punches as the two men grappled on the floor.

Frustrated by Norman's frantic effort to hold him down,

Matt's anger became intense. He reached back and threw a powerful punch to the left side of Norman's face.

Kate screamed.

Blood splattered everywhere.

Norman's body became limp, and he slumped over on his right side.

Matt struggled to his feet. Breathing heavily, his face soaked in perspiration, Matt began to move toward Kate.

He reached into his jacket and pulled out a gun.

Matt held the gun in his right hand and pointed it at Kate.

In a crazed outburst, he yelled, "Where is she? You know what I can do to you. If you don't tell me, I'll make sure you never see her again!"

Kate backed up to the bedroom door in an attempt to block Matt's access.

He continued toward her with a menacing look, the gun still pointed at her head.

Shoving her up against the door, he reached out with his left hand and grabbed her by the throat. He forced her head against the door and began squeezing her neck tightly.

Kate's face turned red.

Unable to speak or breathe.

Matt seethed with anger.

"You bitch! You took her away so I'd never even know she existed. That wasn't fair, Kate. I have rights here."

Suddenly, a noise emanated from the front door.

Matt relaxed his grip on Kate and turned to see Gallagher in the doorway.

With Matt's attention briefly focused on Gallagher, Kate seized the opportunity and slammed both of her hands tightly around Matt's right wrist. Matt attempted to throw her down and free up his gun hand, but his effort failed.

In a heartbeat Gallagher stunned him with a vicious karate chop to the neck.

Matt stumbled but retained control of the gun as he pushed Kate to the floor with his left hand.

Gallagher wasted no time in delivering a sledgehammer punch to Matt's nose.

Weakened and staggering, with blood pouring from his nose, Matt managed to maintain control of the gun.

Gallagher pounded his fist into him again.

Matt grunted out a painful roar and the two men fell to the floor in a desperate struggle for the gun.

Gallagher pinned Matt's right hand to the floor to prevent him from getting off a fatal shot. The struggle continued, but soon the weight and strength advantage of the former football player began to take over. Unable to wrestle the gun from Matt's grasp, Gallagher's eyes began to bulge. His face pounded with increasing pressure as he bore down, gritting his teeth trying to resist Matt's powerful attempt to flip him over.

Nearly out of breath, Gallagher lifted up his right knee and slammed it into Matt's groin.

Matt let out a blood-curdling scream.

Energized by his pain, Matt pulled his hand with the gun toward his body and wedged it against Gallagher's stomach in an attempt to fatally wound his attacker.

The struggle continued.

A shot rang out and reverberated loudly through the room.

The struggle subsided.

Kate looked on in sheer panic.

Gallagher slowly lifted up, revealing his blood-stained clothing.

He crawled to his knees and began to stand up.

Matt Winston's arms slumped to his side.

The gun dropped to the floor.

His mouth sagged open.

His unmoving chest showed an ever-growing red stain as his lifeless body laid motionless on the floor.

Kate scrambled to her feet and immediately went into the bedroom where Hayley could be heard crying.

Gallagher pulled out his cell phone and rushed to Norman's side.

"Are you alright, Norman?"

The left side of Norman's face was bloodied and markedly swollen. Blood trickled from his nose. He took a deep breath and began to speak with a groggy, almost unintelligible voice, "If an IED didn't do me in, one punch certainly won't."

Then he slowly reached up to touch the side of his face, "But, I think my jaw is broken."

Gallagher responded with words of encouragement, "Your call saved them, Norman. If I had gotten here a minute later, it would have been too late."

Norman nodded and then paused for a few seconds.

He looked up at Gallagher.

"Did you kill him?" he asked.

Gallagher said nothing as he looked over at Matt's body and then back to Norman.

Norman read Gallagher's eyes and knew the answer.

"I've got to get some help for you," said Gallagher.

He punched 911 into the keypad of his cell phone.

"We have a medical emergency at 1207 Statler Road. Get here as soon as possible."

Epilogue

The memorial service for Cindy Kraemer was private—restricted to family members and close friends.

The news media stayed a healthy distance away from the small church out of respect for the family's wishes for privacy. But the sensationalism of the dramatic story had not run its course. The public clamored for more sordid details about the criminal plot involving a local news media icon, police corruption, drugs, multiple murders, and the shootout at the miniature-horse farm.

The Townsend police stood guard as a buffer to keep the dozens of cameras and reporters from getting too close.

The service lasted nearly an hour.

So much sadness.

Enough to last a lifetime.

When it was over, the group of forty family members and friends gathered for a reception in a nicely appointed room in an annex to the church. Cindy's mother, Gilda, walked over to Kate who stood with Gallagher and Hayley.

"Can I have a moment alone with you?" she asked.

"Of course," Kate said.

She looked at Gallagher. He nodded and took Hayley's hand.

Hayley tugged at Gallagher's arm and pulled him toward a buffet table covered with fresh fruit and pastries. Norman had wheeled to the end of the table where he filled a cup of coffee from an urn.

Norman turned toward them as they approached.

"Hey—there's the best little girl," he said. "Come on over and give your Uncle Norman a big hug."

He reached out and handed a chocolate chip cookie to Hayley. She took the cookie and offered a bashful smile.

"Come on," he urged as he leaned down toward her.

Hayley stepped closer, reached up and briefly put her arms around his neck.

"Aahhh," said Norman. "Like I said—the best little girl."

He looked up at Gallagher. Norman's eyes grew misty.

"It's been a rough few weeks—very rough," he said.

Gallagher put his hand on Norman's shoulder.

"I know. You've suffered a huge loss. But Norman, they're looking down and smiling at you. You came through—you put your life on the line to save Kate and Hayley—you came through in a big way. I couldn't have pieced this together and found Hayley without you."

Norman shook his head and swallowed hard.

"You're right. I owed it to Don and Cindy."

He paused for a few seconds. Then he looked up.

"I've lost so much, but along the way I think I gained a good friend. Keep in touch, Gallagher. Gonna miss you around here."

"Don't worry, Norman. You'll be hearing from me."

———«(•)»———

Gilda and Kate walked outside and stood near the flower garden.

"You know, after Don passed away, Cindy called me every night," said Gilda. "You had only been in Townsend a few days, but in one of her calls, Cindy told me how wonderful you were with Hayley and how beautifully she responded to you. She said, 'Mom, now that Don is gone, I have to think about appointing a guardian for Hayley. If anything ever happens to me, I know Kate would be a great mother. I want to appoint her.'"

Kate took a deep breath and leaned forward.

She put her hand on Gilda's arm and looked at her with searching eyes.

"My husband and I had Cindy late in life," Gilda continued. "I'm eighty-five years old. How could I raise a three-year old? Hayley needs to grow up with a younger family. I'm her legal guardian now, but I want to respect Cindy's wishes. You're her birth mother—she belongs with you."

They hugged.

Tears flowed.

They walked inside.

Kate leaned down, picked up Hayley and looked at Gallagher.

No words had to be spoken.

He knew.

Three days later, Gallagher, Kate, and Hayley had finished packing and prepared to leave for the airport when Gallagher's cell chimed.

It was Sanchez calling.

"Hey, Gallagher?"

"Yes, Bob."

"Just wanted you to know that the ballistics tests checked out. I can stop by this morning to return your Glock before you leave for Boston."

"Not necessary. You can keep it."

A long pause.

"Really? Giving up on the private eye business? Is this the end?"

Gallagher looked over at Kate and Hayley as they put the finishing touches on another suitcase.

"No, Bob—I wouldn't say 'The End.' It's more like a new beginning."

Acknowledgments

I am deeply indebted to the following people who offered their assistance during the writing of this manuscript:

My preview readers: Kristen Rzezuski, Diane Beane, Michelle Carmody, Lori Gebo, Marcia Stein, and Phyllis Oblas. Thank you for the many hours you devoted to reading and critiquing my book. Your comments have been so helpful. It's great to see that you've become such "Gallagher Junkies."

My technical experts on police protocol: Keith Kaplan of the Boston Police; PO Michael Del Peschio (Ret.) and Pattiann Pavacic-Del Peschio of the City of Yonkers, New York Police Department. Your advice and editing of the police scenes have added to the realism of this novel.

Dr. Kallen Hull who related to me his real-life experience of being attacked by a dog while he was jogging.

Ana and John Turner of Studio 913 for their excellent photography.

Mr. Roger Slobody and his family and staff at Sawmill River Farm in West Brookfield, MA. Thank you for allowing me to visit your farm and for helping me to appreciate the wondrous beauty of miniature horses.

To my friends, family and acquaintances who allowed me to use their names as characters. Remember ... this is fiction! Don't take it personally if you ended up as a bad guy.

My late cousin and business partner, Lan Tauber: His enthusiasm for my writing has always been a true inspiration. He is greatly missed.

My wife, Ronney who puts up with endless nights while I'm lost in front of my computer, but always manages to come up with the right word when I need it.

Mr. L. Edward Purcell for his marvelous editing skills.

My children, Jonathan and Randi: Your loving encouragement makes me strive to become a better writer.

CPSIA information can be obtained
at www.ICGtesting.com
Printed in the USA
LVHW010749080820
662689LV00002B/356